UNTIL THE DAY BREAK

UNTIL THE DAY BREAK

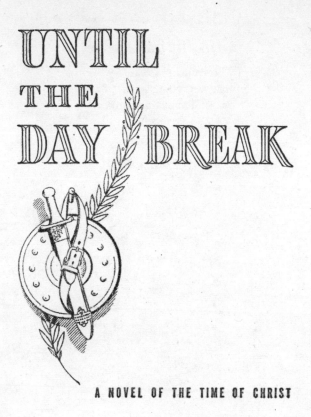

A NOVEL OF THE TIME OF CHRIST

SALLIE LEE BELL

Zondervan Publishing House ... Grand Rapids 2, Mich.

UNTIL THE DAY BREAK

Printed in the United States of America

DEDICATED

To the memory
of my beloved husband
THADDEUS PARK BELL

FOREWORD

This novel does not aim to be a historical novel in the truest sense of the word. A careful effort has been made, however, to preserve the historical sequence of events and to portray the life of the period.

A common offense among interpreters of history has been to attribute to Herod Antipas certain events which belong rightfully to Herod Agrippa. Perhaps the critical historian will pardon the few changes which were made toward the close of the book, for the sake of the story.

SALLIE LEE BELL

CONTENTS

Chapter One

A Woman Wins an Argument

A SHRILL SCREAM ECHOED THROUGH HEROD'S PALACE in Tiberias. Herodias, the wife of the governor, was giving vent to her fury by punishing one of her slaves. The leather lash, tipped with sharp metal, fell upon his bare back, tearing the flesh. Blood trickled from the jagged wounds and the slave, a mere boy, sank in a heap, moaning in agony.

"Mercy! Mercy, mistress!" he cried as once more Herodias raised the lash.

"Mercy!" she echoed harshly. Her eyes blazed and her lips twisted into a thin, hard smile. "If I were not merciful, I'd have you crucified! The next time you dare to laugh at me behind my back you'll get the cross instead of the lash!"

"I wasn't laughing, mistress. I swear I wasn't!" he cried weakly. "Please believe me!" He raised trembling hands to her in a gesture of supplication. "Be merciful! Be merciful, mistress!"

"I'll be merciful this time," she conceded, "but get up and get out of here and keep out of my sight or I may regret that I didn't have you punished as you deserve

1

to be." She turned her back upon him and threw the lash across the room.

The slave limped painfully across the room and through the tapestry-hung doorway, moaning softly to himself.

Herodias dropped wearily upon a near-by divan. Her fury had spent itself, leaving her exhausted from nervous reaction and physical effort. *Perhaps after all,* she mused, *she had been mistaken and had only imagined the boy had been laughing at her. It didn't matter, though. The slaves were gossiping about her and Mara. Of that she was sure, though she couldn't be sure about the boy's laughing at her. Well, this would warn them to be more careful.*

Her smoldering rage stirred to life again as her thoughts revolved around the upsetting revelation which had been the real source of her anger. All of her plans and ambitious schemes were in danger since Herod's roving fancy had been captured by his Jewish slave girl, Mara. The first time Herodias had seen the girl she had realized that her rival was dangerously beautiful, but she had not dreamed that her own ripe charms could be supplanted in Herod's affections by anyone, least of all by a Jewish slave. How humiliating this was to her vanity!

Though Herodias had loved her husband Philip with perhaps the only real love of which she was capable, she had left him eagerly when she had responded to the passionate, stormy wooing of his brother, Herod Antipas, Tetrarch of Galilee.

Herod had lured her with visions which stirred her

ambitions, and together they had plotted to occupy the throne of Palestine. Emissaries who had influence at Rome with the emperor Tiberius had pledged their aid. Spurred by Herodias' ambitions, Herod had later conceived the idea of finally revolting against Rome and setting up a kingdom in Jerusalem with himself as ruler of the Eastern world.

Now these schemes and hopes of hers were in danger of being destroyed because of the slave, Mara.

Herodias rose from the divan and went to Herod's apartments. The afternoon sun shone through an open window and painted the marble columns and soft-tinted walls of the palace room with gold, casting delicate shadows upon the silken curtains and brilliant tapestries that adorned the chamber.

Herod turned a surprised gaze upon her as she entered. She saw that he was none too pleased at her coming and the knowledge only added to her anger. She came to the subject at once.

"I've come to talk to you about Mara," she began. "You're going to have to get rid of that girl. I've made up my mind to it."

He regarded her with a scowl. "What for?"

"Don't pretend you don't know!" she blazed.

His gaze wavered before her brilliant eyes. He realized she knew the truth. He was afraid but he sought to cover his fear.

"I won't do it," he blustered as he began to pace the floor.

She stared moodily at him as he strode back and forth, trying to bolster a courage which experience had told her would weaken rapidly under the fire of her temper and the lash of her tongue. His face, with its high Roman nose, broad forehead and piercing black eyes under the level brows, though already faintly ravaged by the marks of debauchery, was still handsome. It was the face of a conqueror, but Herodias had learned that it masked the soul of a weakling, one who could be swayed by sudden impulses, or fears, or unsatisfied desires.

"Yes, you will," she said quietly. She lay back upon the cushioned couch and looked at him through eyes half closed and hidden by the thick short lashes. "And the sooner you do it, the better it will be for both of us."

"You're quite a prophetess, aren't you?" he remarked sarcastically as he ceased his striding and stood before her.

Herodias suddenly lost her half-mocking manner.

"If I am, then why have you been stupid enough to think that I couldn't see what even the slaves are laughing about behind my back?"

"Why do you concern yourself about my slaves? Being my wife ought to satisfy you. You once thought it would," he retorted with a hint of malice in his voice.

"It does. And I expect to remain your wife. That's why you've got to get rid of Mara." Her tones were cold and incisive.

"I won't be dictated to by you," he stormed. "I paid a good price for that girl and I intend to keep her. What's made you so upset about her all of a sudden?"

"You've made her your concubine, haven't you?" she demanded.

"What if I have? I have others besides her and you haven't objected to them. You knew I had them before I married you."

"Do you think I'm so stupid that I can't see you're in love with the girl? I have no intention of being supplanted by a slave."

Herod laughed loudly, more loudly than was necessary. "The idea of my being in love with my slave! You talk like a fool." Then he added with a sudden return of courage, "Your vile temper and insane jealousy are getting unbearable!"

She approached him and spoke in low measured tones. "You didn't tell me I was unbearable when I was Philip's wife. I was the most marvelous creature in the world when you were trying to steal me from him."

"I was a fool!" he cried. "I didn't know what I was getting when I stole you." He flounced from her like an angry child. "Besides, I satisfied your ambitions. You wanted to be stolen."

She followed him and put an arm about his shoulders. A stab of fear shot through her as he failed to respond to her caresses as he had always done upon the rare occasions when she had bestowed them. She was of the type who reasoned that caresses too generously bestowed lost their value.

"Yes, my Herod, I wanted to be stolen," she murmured as her arm tightened about him, "but neither of us will be satisfied until you sit upon the throne as king of Palestine."

"Be careful!" he cautioned her. "You know it isn't safe to mention such things here! Suppose someone should hear you before we're sure Tiberius is willing?"

"You're afraid, Herod," she murmured softly but with a note of triumph, "afraid of a whispered word. Suppose I should decide to be indiscreet and talk loudly enough for some of Pontius Pilate's spies to hear?"

"Are you trying to threaten me?" he cried furiously but with a note of fear in his voice which did not escape her.

"No," she said with sudden tenderness. "I was only trying to remind you of the ties that bind us together. Can't you understand? I've suffered shame and humiliation to become your wife. I did it because I loved you. You loved me then, Herod. I want to keep that love." Her face was close to his.

"I loved you because I admired your fiery spirit. I didn't know it was going to burn me up!" He jerked himself from her embrace.

Her anger blazed again. "You didn't think about being burned up until this slave attracted you. Do you think that after having endured what I have because of my love for you I'm going to be put aside at the threshold of success? If you don't get rid of the girl, I'll kill her!" Herodias' voice rose shrilly.

He burst forth furiously, "If you dare to harm her, I'll kill you! Mind your own affairs and leave my slaves to me. Mara's going to stay here." There was a note of emphasis in his voice that smote her with a faint fear.

"So it *is* true! You really love her."

"Well, what if I do?" he demanded, feeling that he had a temporary advantage which he meant to keep if he could.

"What if you do?" she repeated slowly. Her face was set in stern lines that robbed it of its beauty. Her eyes blazed with a light that Herod knew only too well. Her body was tense and rigid. "What if Tiberius should learn of that other plot of yours before you are ready to break with Rome? You'd hang on a Roman cross. You'd have time then to think of what you had lost because you had let your passion for a slave make you forget your love for your wife."

"You're jumping at conclusions, my dear," he remonstrated as his manner suddenly became conciliatory. His advantage had vanished and fear again had taken its place. "I haven't forgotten anything. I never said I loved Mara. I don't know where you got such an idea. What is one slave more or less to you?"

"That's just what I'd like to know," she retorted. "What is one slave more or less to you? I demand that you get rid of this girl. If you don't love her, then get rid of her."

He hesitated a moment while her unyielding gaze held his and he felt her power dominating him as it had always done.

"Oh, all right, all right! Have your way," he said resignedly. "You knew you would, all the time."

A satisfied smile flashed across her crimson lips but the smile did not soften her face. It only emphasized the cruel light in her eyes.

"I was only hoping I would. I feel so afraid at the thought of losing you, my husband, so helpless and defenseless against anyone who'd try to take you from me." Her voice was low and meek but Herod knew that she was only acting.

"Defenseless! Ha!" he cried hoarsely. "A woman's tongue can put to shame any weapon ever invented."

"You'll get rid of her at once?" she asked softly, ignoring his thrust.

"Anything for peace!" he submitted. "I'll send her away where she won't bother you any longer, but I won't sell her to anyone else. I'll keep her, if only to show you that I'm master of my own household."

She smiled at his childish bluster as she said, "We won't argue about that."

"Thank the gods for that!" he groaned. "I've had enough arguments for the present."

"So have I," she agreed, a note of weariness in her voice.

"Of course, now that you've had your own way. Have the kindness to leave," he said sullenly, as he turned from her and seated himself.

Her dark eyes rested upon him with a gaze that baffled him and he stared at her moodily as she turned to leave. Her abundant black hair fell in rippling waves down her back. Herod had once wanted her more than anything else on earth. Now the desire for her had waned and she was like a weight around his neck. The guilty secret of rebellion they shared forced him to keep her until his ambitions were attained. After that he would find a way to get rid of her.

A parting of the curtains roused him from his bitter reverie. He looked up and saw Mara. The sunlight fell in a golden shaft upon her slender figure. Her long fair hair glistened like burnished gold with glints of red. It was caught loosely back from her face by a band of gold set with topazes. Her eyes, big and brown, were shaded by long, curving lashes. Her features were small and delicately chiseled. She wore a pale yellow garment that glittered and sparkled with amber crystal trimmings.

Herod sat for a moment and stared at her as she stood waiting for him to bid her enter. How lovely she was!

He shook a finger at her. "You were listening behind that curtain."

"I couldn't help it, master. You sent for me and I was waiting until you were alone." Her voice was low and mellow.

"It's a good thing you did wait and that Herodias didn't discover us together." He sighed. "I'm no match for that tongue of hers."

"The lady Herodias hates me," Mara murmured regretfully.

"She has reason to. You heard what she said. Now that she's found out the truth, I'll have to send you away."

"Please don't do that, master!" she begged, stepping closer and raising appealing eyes.

"I'm afraid to keep you here. I don't trust Herodias. She'd kill you, just as she threatened to, if I did. Will you be sorry to leave me, Mara?" he asked with a new note of tenderness in his voice.

"How can you ask, master, when you know the answer?"

He took her in his arms and crushed her to him. "You

do love me, don't you, my beautiful one?" he murmured, burying his face in her perfumed hair.

She raised a slender hand and caressed his cheek. "How could I help loving a man so kind and so handsome as Herod?" she replied.

He kissed her possessively. "You're flattering me, but I love to hear it from your lips. Herodias has cause to be jealous of you, for I swear I love you more than I ever thought I could love any woman. I'm not going to let you go for long. I promise you that."

"I'm glad of that, master." She sighed.

"Would you like to be a queen, Mara?" he asked impulsively.

"A *queen?*" she echoed. "What do you mean?"

"You heard what Herodias and I were saying, didn't you?"

"But I didn't understand," she said cautiously.

"Don't try to," he advised with a sudden return of fear. "Just be patient and keep on loving me and some day you may understand."

"How could I stop loving you?" She sighed, then added naively, "I would love to be a queen—if you were my king."

He laughed and kissed her again. "So would Herodias. That's why she's so furious about you. She's not willing to take any chances, so I'll have to send you away, at least until her suspicions are forgotten. I shall send you to your sister in Jerusalem. You may take Hannah with you to look after you; then as soon as Herodias gets over this fit of jealousy or I find a way to make her consent to your return, I shall send for you."

"I hope it will be soon!" she exclaimed as she put her arms about his neck and her warm, eager lips sought his.

When she had left him she paused for a moment in the corridor, thinking of what he had said. She had understood more of Herod's conversation with Herodias than she had admitted. Herodias' hint of their plot had opened her eyes to a new vision and his words to her gave her hope that Herodias would be cast aside and she would take her place. It was what she had dreamed of and yet had never dared to believe possible.

"Just think of it! I'd be a queen!" she said aloud with a gurgling little laugh.

"That's a dangerous word for a slave to use." A mocking voice spoke at her side.

She turned startled eyes upon Nereus, a palace guard, a handsome swaggering fellow clad in a tight-fitting tunic with a short mantle of rust-colored satin falling from his broad shoulders. Her eyes hardened. She hated Nereus for his stealthy, annoying pursuit of her, his cocksureness, his superior air, yet she feared him, for she sensed that he had some secret influence with Herodias which gave him the self-assurance so unusual in a palace guard.

"What are you doing here?" she asked.

"If it's of any importance to you, I'm on my way to see your mistress," he replied. "Now, what are you doing here, murmuring foolish words about being a queen?"

"It's none of your affair," she answered as fear crept over her because of the slip she had made.

" 'I would love to be a queen'!" he mimicked. "Herodias might be interested in hearing those words."

Panic seized her. What if he should tell Herodias? She turned away without replying and started to leave but he stopped her.

"Wait, my haughty queen," he said, catching hold of her and pulling her toward him. "Don't leave me in anger." His arms closed about her.

"Let me go!" she cried, struggling in his grasp.

"Not without a kiss, most beautiful," he said mockingly.

"How dare you! Let me go!" She tried again to release herself.

"How dare I? What words for a slave to use in addressing a soldier of Rome!"

"I'm not your slave and you have no right to treat me like this," she flashed.

"Do you think you're the first of Herod's slaves to be kissed by a soldier?" he taunted.

"Whether I am or not, I don't want your kisses. Let me go!"

"So you don't want my kisses. Many a slave as beautiful as you has given her lips willingly to me."

"Go and kiss some of those willing ones," she retorted.

"You were not so arrogant a few months back, before Herod began to notice you," he reminded her.

"If you don't let me go, I'll call Herod and he'll have you flogged!" she cried as she struggled in futile anger.

"Don't be too sure about that," he advised. "You're not a queen yet, you know, and there's many a slip between the slave block and the throne."

With a laugh at her blazing anger he let her go and watched her as she ran down the marble-paved hall.

Little fool! he mused. *She's getting ideas, just as I thought. Watch your step, Nereus. Things may yet work out your way, if you'll only have patience and use your wits.*

Chapter Two

Two Schemers Meet

WITH SURPRISING SELF-ASSURANCE IN A PALACE GUARD, Nereus entered Herodias' apartment. She was waiting for him, lounging gracefully upon a low couch. Around her were bright-hued cushions, a clever setting for her dark beauty.

"You sent for me, my lady," he said, bowing low.

"Yes. Sit down," she invited. "I've had a talk with Herod. What you told me is true, Nereus. Herod is in love with Mara."

There was a smile playing about the corners of his mouth. How wise he had been to use his eyes and ears!

She reached out and touched his lean brown hand with her slender fingers. "You've always been such a helpful friend." She sighed. "I'm so deeply grateful. I never shall forget it. I couldn't get along without you."

He seized her hand in a crushing grasp and his eyes glowed with sudden fire. "More than your friend," he stated. "Never forget that. You seem to want to forget that I love you and live only to serve you."

She withdrew her hand and spoke rather petulantly. "What a tangled web of disappointment and thwarted desires life is! You love me and I am bound to Herod by ties that I'm not willing to break and Herod has forgotten me for the charms of a slave." Her full red lips were drawn into a pout.

"Herod is a fool to forget you for anyone. I'd give all the joys of Olympus to know that you were mine."

"Of course he's a fool," she agreed morosely, ignoring his last remark, "but that doesn't help the situation."

She leaned nearer and her eyes grew bright with the sudden hard light that flashed in their dark depths.

"There's something I want you to do for me, Nereus—something I couldn't trust anyone else to do. Will you do it for me?"

"Haven't I always served you?" His hand once more closed over hers. His eyes held her gaze and in their depths there was something which frightened her while it lured her. It had always been so, since she had first known him. There was some inner force which drew her to him, yet which filled her with subtle fear.

"Yes, you have," she replied. "But I've often wondered if it was entirely because of your professed love for me or for your own sake. Every time you did a favor for me you had me more completely in your debt. Sometimes ambition is stronger than love."

He smiled to himself. How true that was of her!

"My only ambition is to serve you," he murmured. "Just remember that and that I have served you faithfully." He kissed the tips of her fingers.

"If you please me in this," she smiled and carressed his bronzed cheek lightly, "I shall be more deeply in your debt than ever. I've persuaded Herod to send the girl away. He's sending her to Jerusalem, but only for a time. He won't get rid of her, but I'm determined that she shall not come back here. I want you to help me keep her from returning."

"How?" There was a note of suspicion in his voice.

"She mustn't live to return." A bitter note emphasized each word. "I want you to follow her to Jerusalem and plan some way to get rid of her before Herod grows impatient and sends for her."

"You mean murder, Herodias?" His eyes were like points of steel.

"Don't be stupid! Is it murder when a political offender is destroyed? Tiberius wouldn't call it that; neither would Herod."

"I understand," but there was no warmth in his voice.

"Thanks. I thought you would. But, remember, you mustn't do anything that would make Herod suspect me. If he did, the gods themselves couldn't protect me from his anger." She laughed mirthlessly.

"What if he should suspect me? If he misses me and anything happens to Mara during my absence, he'd be likely to suspect me."

"You're clever enough to take care of yourself," she replied indifferently. "I don't think you'll do anything to endanger your own head."

"In other words, I must look out for myself," he remarked as his hold upon her hand loosened.

She leaned toward him, and her arm stole about his neck. She was quick to sense the meaning of that loosened grasp of his hand.

"If I thought there would be danger for you, I wouldn't

send you," she murmured in a rich, husky voice. "But I know how clever you are. You won't fail me, will you, my dear Nereus?"

"I shall try not to." Then with a faintly mocking note, "I shall try to do your bidding, my queen."

He seized her suddenly, almost roughly, and held her to him, but swiftly she raised her hand as a barrier between their lips.

"Your queen, Nereus?" She spoke a little sadly from behind the barrier. "No, my dear. Sometimes I wish it could be. But I shall be Herod's queen or die in the effort. I've dreamed and schemed and fought to accomplish this and may the gods have mercy upon anyone who dares to stand in my way!"

"As you said, ambition is a stronger master than love," he remarked as he still held her.

"But I love Herod," she said as she released herself.

"And I love you," he retorted. "There's a difference, though, in our love. You seek to put Herod on a throne so that you may satisfy your own ambition. I seek only to serve you with the hope of making you happy."

"I wonder . . ." she speculated as she gazed into his eyes.

"Of course there's always the hope that one day your heart may turn to the stronger love." He smiled as he kissed the tips of her fingers again.

Chapter Three

A Strange Encounter

It was early morning when Mara and her servant Hannah set out on horseback to Jerusalem, accompanied by a small detachment of Herod's guard. They went by way of Caesarea, along the great highway that skirted the seacoast. Mara had chosen the longer way because she had never taken that route.

The journey was a thrilling experience to her. It was like a breath of freedom after long confinement in a luxurious prison.

When Mara was still a small child, her sister Rachel had married Samuel, a prosperous merchant, and had moved to Jerusalem. Shortly afterward her father, Aaron, a ne'er-do-well, had accepted a menial position in the service of the despised Roman government and had taken her and her mother from their home in Bethany to Tiberias. In Tiberias they were despised by the Galilean Jews as well as the Gentiles who were their neighbors.

Mara's mother, crushed in spirit and broken in health, had died, leaving Mara to the mercies of a father who cared nothing for her and, which was worse, had ceased to care that he was a son of Abraham.

When she was old enough for her beauty to attract attention, Aaron had sold her to Herod. Though Mara was not consulted, she was rather pleased at the change. Her life had been sordid and unhappy and she welcomed anything that promised her something different. She had heard of the magnificence of Herod's palace and his extravagant luxury and slavery in such surroundings held no terrors for her. She was scarcely old enough to realize her degradation in the eyes of all true Jews or of the outrage she was committing against all the sacred traditions of her people by belonging to this Gentile ruler.

By the time Herod began to tire of Herodias and Mara's ripening beauty attracted his roving fancy, she had become schooled in the deceit and scheming of court life. She was flattered, and she exulted in the knowledge that she was the favorite of her master.

They passed along the edge of the beautiful plain of Sharon where scarlet poppies made gay splashes of color and marigolds raised feathery puffs of yellow to a golden sun, where dwarf cornflowers spread a blue carpet which was sprinkled with star points of white narcissus, where grapevines were putting forth their crumpled, pale green leaves, where the potter sat at his lowly task with his flattened thumb molding water pots and cooking utensils for the poorer families.

Many times her thoughts returned to that conversation she had overheard. One day perhaps Herod would be king of all this land. And she would be his queen! The thought thrilled her every time she recalled Herod's words to her. She knew nothing of the intrigue by which

Herod hoped to gain his kingdom, of the long months of scheming, plotting and bribery he had already spent. She was concerned only about the future. A faint fear seized her when she thought of Herodias. Herodias had threatened to kill her and Herodias was relentless and resourceful. But Herod loved her and he would protect her. Herodias had only fanned the flame of that love by making him send her away.

Mara didn't love Herod. At times she feared him and at others she loathed him, but he had been kind to her despite his cruelty and uncertain temper, and the hope of supplanting Herodias had lured and thrilled her.

As they rode past Lydda the way became more rugged and their horses were forced to a slower pace. A few miles from Jerusalem Herod's escort left them. As Mara watched them disappear in the distance, with bright armor shining and the thud of hoofs growing fainter, mingled emotions swept over her.

In the late afternoon, as the dying sun gilded the distant mountain peaks, they skirted the last high hill that stood between them and the Holy City. Mara stopped her horse a moment and looked about her. The sycamore trees, with their bright green leaves, were waving gently in the breeze. Farther on were fields of young corn, waving pale streamers that heralded a bountiful harvest. To the right a flock of sheep were responding to the shepherd's call of "ta-a-a-a-ho-o-o-o." As they watched, the sheep milled about him and then started slowly for the fold.

"Look, Hannah! Isn't that beautiful?" she cried, and then she began to sing in a low voice, " 'The Lord is my shepherd: I shall not want.'" She laughed as she finished the Psalm. "That sounds queer, doesn't it, coming from my lips? I had forgotten I knew it until I saw that shepherd." Her face became suddenly serious. "This place affects me strangely, Hannah."

"That's what it should do to any true daughter of Israel," Hannah said solemnly.

"But I'm not a true daughter of Israel any longer." A tinge of sadness crept into her voice.

"I would to God you were!" exclaimed Hannah fervently.

The Jew's religious fervor, intense patriotism and hatred of the Romans—these Hannah possessed in their full power.

As they rounded a curve in the road the Holy City came into full view, rising from the plain and resting upon the hills like a cluster of white gems on a green velvet background. Beyond it rose the Mount of Olives, sloping upward from the Valley of Jehoshaphat. To the south of them lay the Vale of Hinnom mantled by long shadows. At its southern extremity towered the Hill of Evil Counsel, standing above like a grim sentinel.

The city itself held Mara's eye. It was the first time she had ever seen it and its beauty and magnificence enthralled her. The Temple, glistening white in the sunlight, stood out above all, more magnificent than any of the high-towered buildings within the massive walls. The smoke rose in thin spirals from the court. Presently there was the sound of silver trumpets as the priests blew their threefold blasts upon them, signifying that the day's work was ended.

" 'Lift up your heads, O ye gates; even lift them up, ye everlasting doors; and the King of Glory shall come in,' " murmured Hannah reverently, her eyes bright with tears.

The King of Glory! What a contrast the memory of Herod made. Sudden revulsion swept over Mara, banishing her feeling of exaltation.

As they continued on their way a little party of men came toward them on foot. They pulled their horses to one side to let them pass. The leader of the band wore an outer coat of camel's skin. It fitted his figure loosely and was held in at the waist with a leather girdle. He carried a staff like those used by mountain climbers. His face was the color of bronze. His dark beard and flowing hair framed aquiline features.

His companions were men of the poorer class, but each bore upon his countenance the unmistakable stamp of the full-blooded Jew. No trace of despised alien blood had entered to mar the pure strain that flowed in their veins.

Mara watched them with interest. As she turned to continue her journey, she found herself looking into a pair of deep brown eyes that held her gaze. She had not noticed this man, the last of the group, until she was face to face with him. He seemed like a mere boy in contrast with the others. His strong, sunburned face and athletic figure would have compelled attention from anyone, but she forgot everything else when she met his frank gaze. He had stopped in front of her and was staring at her in rapt, wide-eyed admiration.

Mara returned his stare, thrilled and breathless. He

was the first to recover. With a startled movement of embarrassment he turned and followed his companions. She turned toward the city but paused a moment and looked back to catch a last look at him. He had stopped and was looking back at her.

She couldn't repress a giggle as she caught up with Hannah.

"I wonder who he is," she remarked, a lilt in her voice.

"He has the air of a holy man and he must have lived in the wilderness because he's so sunburned and he's wearing skins," replied Hannah.

"You know very well I didn't mean that wild-looking man in front. I meant the last one, the young one."

"Nobody important or he wouldn't be the last of the line."

A brief silence followed.

"Hannah, did you see how he looked at me?" Mara couldn't repress the excitement which crept into her voice.

Hannah smiled. "I'm not blind, little mistress," she said tenderly. "But it's a good thing Herod didn't see the way he stared at you. He'd have him flogged for his impertinence."

"No one ever looked at me like that before," Mara exclaimed eagerly. "Other men have admired me, but their every look was an insult. Why was it so different, Hannah?"

Hannah hesitated a moment and her voice was very solemn as she replied. "The look you saw in the eyes of those men in Galilee came from hearts that were full of lust. The look that boy gave you came from the heart of someone who could love you well enough to make you his wife and not his mistress."

"I understand," answered Mara in a voice grown heavy with sadness.

Silently they entered the gates of the city.

Chapter Four

Within the Gates

As they rode through the massive gateway with its square stone towers, Mara brought her horse to a walk and looked about her eagerly. The Roman guard was changing watch with the clank of armor and the flash of spears. The shops were closing and those who lived outside the city were going toward the gates.

She and Hannah passed on through Valley Street that led toward the Golden Gate. A group of cheese-mongers hurried past with their heavily-laden donkeys, clucking to their beasts and talking rapidly in their queer dialect, a curious blend of many tongues.

A dozen Bedouins clattered by, bound for the Damascus Gate. They urged their horses to a dangerous pace down the narrow, white-paved street, cursing and gesticulating at the slow-footed pedestrians who blocked their path.

They came to the Market Place, the center of a noisy throng, a chaos of voices shouting in many dialects. Two Essenes, with their garments of undyed wool, walked slowly toward the Valley Gate, conversing quietly, seemingly unconscious of the glances of amusement or curiosity bent upon them. A Pharisee approaching from the opposite direction cast a glance of disdain upon those who obstructed his way and drew haughtily aside for fear his garment would touch them and be defiled. The Jews made way for him and bowed respectfully as he continued on his way, wearing on his left arm, fastened by a broad leather strap, his phylactery, or tephillim, a large metal capsule which contained extracts from Exodus and Deuteronomy and in which the sacred Name of Jehovah appeared twenty-three times. He presented a curious contrast to the poorer people of the Market Place with their cheap clothing. He walked with pompous stride, his long one-piece outer coat with its blue border and deep fringe fluttering about his heels. As he passed Hannah, she bowed reverently.

"Why did you do that?" Mara asked with a smile of amusement.

"Because he's a holy man. I was taught to show all Pharisees reverence."

"Bah! They're no better than anyone else. Why should you show them reverence just because they know more of the Law than you do? It's silly, I think."

"That's the voice of Herod speaking, little mistress. You are as much a Gentile as your master." Hannah reproved her.

"Perhaps so." Mara shrugged. "But why bother about it?"

A herd of sheep and calves were being driven noisily past them on a crossing street.

"I wonder where they're going," Mara remarked.

"They're being taken to the Temple for sacrifice," Hannah explained.

Mara had forgotten the Temple since she had entered the city. She looked up toward Mount Moriah and saw it shining white against the sky. The girl was stirred. It was the pride of her people. It was the symbol of the tie that had held them together through their periods of suffering, defeat and exile. After absence from the Temple no Jew could gaze upon it without emotion. Though built by a Gentile and profaned by the Roman eagle, it was still the center and inspiration of Israel's religion and the seal of her nationality.

After questioning several passers-by, Hannah and Mara found Rachel's house. It was a home of the better class, built squarely and solidly of undressed stone, covered with a glistening coat of whitewash. From the outside a stairway led to the flat roof. Around the roof ran a wide balustrade, and one end of the roof was covered with an arbor over which an evergreen vine trailed.

On each side of the door were two elaborately-carved windows with screens of latticework. A mezuzah hung upon the doorpost in a shining metal case. A mezuzah hung upon the doorpost of every true child of Israel and was the symbol of Jehovah's promise of protection.

They stopped before the door and dismounted. Mara knocked timidly. A porter appeared in answer and stood waiting for them to announce their names, peering at them through the lattice of the door.

"Is this the home of Rachel of Bethany, the wife of Samuel the merchant?" she asked.

"Yes, she lives here," the porter replied, eyeing her solemnly.

"Tell her that her sister has come to pay her a visit."

The porter opened the door and invited them to enter. As they passed within, Hannah paused a moment and reverently touched the mezuzah. She kissed the finger that had touched it, repeating a part of the Scripture which was written on a small scroll in the metal capsule.

They followed the porter into the inner court. Trees and shrubs were grouped picturesquely about. Long beds bordered with narcissus, crocuses and violets were separated by dull-colored brick walks. The narcissus were in bloom and their sweet fragrance mingled with the scent of violets.

They passed on to one of the inner rooms, a large room with massive lounges covered with tapestry woven in many brilliant colors. In the center of the room stood a beautifully-carved table holding upon its polished surface a four-branched candlestick of burnished brass.

In a few moments Rachel came. She stood for a while looking at Mara, then advanced toward her with outstretched arms.

"It really is you!" she exclaimed. "I couldn't believe it. O Mara! I'm so glad!"

As she put her arms around the girl and hugged her almost roughly, Mara felt the sting of tears in her eyes. Any doubts she may have had concerning her welcome were dispelled.

"I know you're tired from that long trip," Rachel said presently. "After you've rested I want you to meet Samuel and the children. They'll be home in a little while."

An hour later they were gathered in the dining room

for the evening meal. Rachel's husband Samuel, a small dark man, gave his guest a cordial welcome. Mara saw Rachel's children for the first time, Miriam, a girl of fourteen who resembled Mara somewhat, and Joseph, her younger brother, a slender, delicate-looking boy who had his father's features.

During the meal, as Mara talked with them and saw the bond of love that united the little group, a new chord was touched in her heart and an unfamiliar, undefined longing stirred within her. She had never been in a home like this and its contrast to her early life with her harsh, drunken father and her crushed, heartbroken mother, and her subsequent life in Herod's palace, wakened a faint regret within her. She felt that she had missed a beautiful part of life. A yearning for the quiet happiness of such a home as this assailed her.

When the meal was finished and thanks had been given, Samuel recited the creed. Joseph stood and joined him, his clear childish treble mingling with the deeper tones of Samuel's voice. Afterward they went into the courtyard. Samuel recounted the day's happenings while Mara sat a silent listener, her hand clasped in Rachel's. She was happier tonight, with a quiet peace and content, than she had ever been. What a contrast it was to the life that surrounded her in Galilee!

When she went to her room she found Hannah waiting for her.

"Hannah, this place has done something to me," she said. "For the first time in my life I feel that I really am a daughter of Abraham and I'm glad of it. I almost wish I were in Rachel's place."

"Would to God you were, my child!" Hannah cried fervently.

When she was almost asleep her eyes flew open suddenly and she stared before her in the darkness. A low laugh burst from her lips.

What a dunce I was to look back at him! I wonder if he felt as silly as I did. I wonder if I'll ever see him again. She sighed as she closed her eyes once more. *What difference would it make whether I did or not?*

In another part of the city Nereus was already asleep. He had come by the shorter route and had arrived ahead of Mara. The task ahead of him was not a pleasant one but he was determined to accomplish it. He was determined to become indispensable to Herodias. He clung with stubborn tenacity to the hope he had so long cherished—that after she had tired of kings and thrones and satisfied ambitions, she would come at last to him.

Chapter Five

A Conversation Brings Regrets

THE NEXT MORNING MARA WAKENED UNUSUALLY early. She dressed and went up on the roof. The breath of flowers was in the air and the smell of freshly-dug earth came from the fields beyond the city walls.

A caravan had already set forth from the Damascus Gate and was raising a cloud of dust. She watched it pass the rocky hill beyond the city gate. It was a queer-looking hill, grotesquely resembling a skull lying there by the roadside. This must be the hill of execution—Golgotha. Hannah had told her about it.

The Praetorium, with its four square towers, cut a sharp outline against the sky. The Tower of Hippicus, guarding the Garden Gate, rose above the wide brick walls, while not far away the Tower of Phaeselis stood, a grim beacon to the wayfarer. Glistening white in the early sun was the palace of Herod the Great. How her people had loathed that despot who had slaughtered, so it seemed, for the pleasure of seeing Jewish blood flow! She remembered stories she had heard concerning him. Would they loathe Herod Antipas equally if he became king? Well, why shouldn't they? He was a Roman and they hated all Romans with a bitter hatred.

She sat and leaned against the balustrade. On this morning Herod and his schemes seemed far away, a part of some vague, half-forgotten dream. Mara fell to wondering what her life would have been if she had never been sold into slavery. Perhaps, had this been so, she would now have a home like Rachel's and children she adored. The face of the boy she had encountered outside the gate flashed before her. A sigh escaped her. Life could have been so different! But it was too late now to think of what might have been.

The sound of trumpets came across the housetops. Mara turned toward the Temple. It was even more beautiful in the morning light. She could see its broad porches, its marble columns, the wide steps and the massive walls surrounding it. Smoke curled from the courts. She remembered the animals she had seen on their way to be slaughtered and burned upon the altar. Why was it that blood must be shed to atone for sin? Why must an innocent victim be sacrificed for a sin-stained person, unfit to come before God?

A sudden arresting thought smote her. For the first time in all her life she viewed herself through the eyes of her people. There was no atonement in their religion for her, no sacrifice that could cleanse the stain of her life. Murder and theft and crime of every kind had their laws of atonement and their avenues of sacrifice that led back to God, but for one like herself the way was closed. For the woman of the streets there was, in the Law of Moses, no way, no hope—only death by stoning. The thought appalled her. The Temple that she had thought so beautiful became abhorrent, a cold, merciless judgment place. She turned away, her eyes clouded with sudden sadness.

The summons to breakfast came and she shrugged her shoulders with an air of defiance as she turned to go below. What difference should the Temple make to her? If she was cut off forever from it, she'd make the best of what life had to offer. She'd find happiness somehow. She wouldn't worry about what she couldn't help.

When the meal was finished and the various morning duties had been attended to, Rachel took her out into the courtyard and they sat in the shade of the trees.

"Now we can have a nice long talk," Rachel said. "Tell me all about yourself. How did you manage to get Herod's consent to make this visit?"

Mara laughed. "I was sent away without being asked. Herodias hates me so much that she made Herod send me away."

"If she hates you so much, it's a wonder she didn't kill you. From the things I've heard about her, I don't think she'd stop at anything."

"She might have tried if she hadn't been afraid of Herod. She's terribly jealous of me, because she knows that Herod's in love with me," Mara declared with a note of pride in her voice that Rachel did not miss.

"That's nothing to be proud of," exclaimed Rachel impulsively.

"No, I—don't—suppose you would think so," Mara faltered.

Rachel regretted her hasty words and hastened to say, "If Herod loves you, I suppose it does make your life a little easier."

"Of course it does. I'm envied by every slave in the palace."

"Do you love Herod, my dear?" asked Rachel with a little catch in her voice.

"No, I don't," answered Mara slowly. "In the beginning I tried to think I did, because I wanted to. But I never could love him."

"You poor child!" murmured Rachel sympathetically. "What a horrible life for you!"

"I don't think so. It's the best life I've ever known. After Mother died it was terrible at home with Father. Herod has been kind to me. It hasn't been horrible at all. I've enjoyed it."

"But, Mara, hasn't the thought of your degradation ever worried you? It almost broke my heart when I learned that Father had sold you to Herod. Don't you realize that your position makes you worse than an outcast?"

"Why am I so great an outcast?" Mara demanded with sudden spirit. "Doesn't the custom of our people allow concubinage? There are thousands of Jewish girls living the same life I live, right here in Jerusalem."

"That may be true. But it doesn't alter the Law of Moses. Men have their concubines, but that doesn't make the concubine any less an outcast, a creature of shame."

Mara was silent for a moment. Then she spoke in low tones from lips that trembled. "You forget that I was sold without having any voice in the matter."

"You were old enough to have rebelled against it."

"Yes, I was. But at the time it seemed the easiest way

out of a miserable existence. I never regretted it until now. This morning, for the first time, I realized the truth. But since I can't undo the past, I won't cry about it. I'll be happy in the present and let the future take care of itself."

She spoke in a reckless voice but there was a tremor in it that Rachel heard and the hot tears stung her eyes.

"My poor little Mara! I'm glad our sweet mother is dead. It would break her heart if she knew about you."

"If she had lived, she would have taught me all she taught you and I would have killed myself rather than submit to the life I'm living. Tell me about her, Rachel. There is so little that I can remember of her."

"She was even more beautiful than you are and everyone who knew her loved her."

"Did she love my father very much?"

"She must have, to have endured the shame and sorrow he caused her."

"A love like that is past my understanding."

"That's because you've never been in love," replied Rachel as a tender smile flitted across her face.

"Then I hope I'll never be the victim of any such foolish passion!" exclaimed Mara fervently.

Rachel laughed but her face suddenly sobered as she said quietly, while a great ache filled her heart, "So do I."

A strained silence fell between them.

"Mother met our father on the Joppa Road, didn't she?" Mara asked presently.

"Yes. It was very romantic. They met outside the Valley Gate. He fell in love with her then and made her acquaintance through a friend."

Mara's eyes were fastened upon a clump of violets but she didn't see them. She was looking, in fancy, into a pair of brown eyes that spoke their ardent admiration.

"What a strange coincidence," she murmured.

"What do you mean?" asked Rachel, her curiosity aroused by the tone of Mara's voice.

"I—I—was thinking of something that happened yesterday on the Joppa Road," Mara stammered in confusion.

"Tell me about it," Rachel urged.

She told Rachel of the meeting outside the gate, and laughed as she spoke of her embarrassment when she turned back to look and found the stranger doing the same thing. Rachel was silent and there was no responsive laughter, but a pained look in her eyes and a greater pain in her heart.

"Rachel," asked Mara suddenly from the silence that followed, "isn't there any way that I could obtain my freedom, if I wanted it?"

"None that I know of, but the death of Herod. If you were only his slave, perhaps we could persuade him to let us purchase your freedom. I was hoping to do that in the beginning, but since you're his concubine, you know there's no release, even though he lost interest in you."

"Then I may as well be satisfied with my lot," she said with forced cheerfulness, "so let's talk about something else."

Rachel changed the subject and Mara tried to appear interested, but over their chatter lay a dark shadow that refused to be dispelled. Rachel sensed the shadow and was troubled by it.

"In a few days," she said, "the Baptist will return to Judea. At least that's what I've heard. Everyone's been talking about him, since he was here not long ago. I heard he passed through the city yesterday."

"Who is he?" asked Mara without interest.

"No one knows, except that he's a great preacher. He appeared suddenly, preaching and baptizing. He calls himself 'The voice of one crying in the wilderness.' Some think he's the Messiah. How I wish he were!"

Mara laughed scornfully. "The *Messiah!* Surely our people aren't still looking for a Messiah! I thought that hope had died long ago. Hannah still babbles about it, but I thought it was because she was old and didn't have better sense."

Rachel stared at her in grieved surprise. "How could you think we could ever forget or cease to hope? Don't you know that every woman of Judea hopes that she may be the mother of the Messiah?"

"Why should the plaything of Herod remember any hope concerning the Messiah?" asked Mara with sudden bitterness.

"Forgive me, my dear. I forgot," Rachel said contritely.

She made an effort to distract Mara's thoughts and blundered again.

"We'll visit the city tomorrow and see all the public buildings. We'll go to the Temple first, because I know you'll want to see that first of all."

"There's no place for me in the Temple!" Mara cried in a strained voice. "Why should I want to visit it?"

Rachel was silent. She did not know what to say.

Chapter Six

A Glimpse at a Riverside

AFTER THAT FIRST DISQUIETING INTERVIEW, MARA WAS happy in Rachel's home. Rachel tried to keep her sister occupied with things outside herself. She had wisely avoided further reference to the subject that rested so heavily upon her heart. She kept the truth about Mara from her friends and evaded their questions concerning her. She knew that if any of them suspected that Mara was a concubine of the hated Herod, both she and Mara would be ostracized.

They went riding often in Rachel's carriage. It was a crude affair with huge wooden wheels and two low seats suspended on leather straps and a higher one in front for the driver. Rachel's pride and the source of many an envious glance, the carriage was one of the few in the city. The sisters visited the shops and Mara enjoyed buying rare new fabrics and costly trinkets for herself and Miriam.

One day a courier came from Herod with a package containing a gift and a message of love for Mara. It gave her a brief thrill of triumph and helped to banish the little cloud that had threatened to mar her peace of mind. It gave her the assurance that Herodias had not yet succeeded in making Herod forget her. Life still had its compensations.

Each day, like a relentless shadow, Nereus followed her, but at a safe distance. He knew that if Mara should see him, his task would be doubly difficult, for she would suspect his presence in Jerusalem. As the sisters left the city on one of their drives, he saw that they were taking the road to Jericho. He remembered that there was a place not far from the city where a hill, covered by a thick undergrowth, overhung the road. An arrow shot from there would find its mark and pursuit or discovery would be impossible.

He got his bow and arrows and took a short-cut which led over the hills. He reached the place before the slower-moving carriage arrived. As it rounded the curve, Mara was an easy target for she sat on the side nearest him and was half turned toward him where he was concealed in the bushes. He raised the bow and deftly placed an arrow. His finger curved about the string to let it fly when suddenly a muttered oath escaped his lips and his hold upon the string loosened while the arrow fell to the ground with a soft thud.

That's murder, you fool! He admonished himself. *Herod would know at once by whose orders it had been done. And you'd pay the penalty for your stupidity.*

Furious with himself for his stupidity and fuming with disappointment and impatience, he mounted his horse and returned to the city. Something must be done soon or Herodias would grow impatient.

As he trotted slowly along an idea came to him. He

couldn't shoot the girl but perhaps he could arrange an accident which would kill her. Why hadn't he thought of it before! The wheels of Rachel's carriage were heavy and clumsy and they were fastened to the axle by one small wooden pin. If that pin should break at just the right spot, the occupants of the carriage might be killed. That spot would have to be chosen carefully. The scheme would require patience and careful planning and it might fail, but it was worth trying. Anything was better than sitting on the outside stairway of Rachel's home as he had been doing, listening and spying night after night with no hope of getting nearer his goal.

Nereus returned that night to the outside stairway, and came back again, spending long hours there listening to conversation which drifted to him through open windows or from the garden, darting into shadows at the approach of someone, in constant fear of discovery, but doggedly determined not to give up until he heard something which might be to his advantage. At last his patience was rewarded. He heard Mara and Rachel planning another ride for the following day. They planned to visit a friend of Rachel's who lived near Emmaus. Nereus smiled as he listened. They were going over the Joppa Road. That road was hilly and there were many sharp curves on it. It would suit his scheme perfectly.

During the night he managed to get the pin out of the front wheel of the carriage and cut it halfway through. The split would not be apparent to the casual observer, but it would make the pin break under a sudden strain. Nervously he waited for the sisters to set out. He watched them from a distance to be sure they took the

Joppa Road and then he turned down another street and outdistanced them before they reached the city gate.

As he trotted along the road he examined carefully each vantage point overlooking a curve, trying to find one not too far away, lest the pin break before they reached the place, yet seeking one which would answer his purpose most perfectly. At last he found the spot. On one side rose the rocky hillside with its scant shrubbery; on the other the road dropped suddenly to the valley below. Anyone thrown over the side of that steep drop would either be killed or crippled for life. And Herod had no fancy for crippled or disfigured slaves.

Nereus tied his horse out of sight and concealed himself in the shrubbery where he waited impatiently for the approach of Mara and Rachel. He saw them coming, finally, the slave lolling over the reins, the sisters laughing and talking, the carriage bumping and careening over the uneven road.

As they drew near he took out a sling, fitted a stone into the leather and let the stone fly. It struck the horse nearer him and the animal started forward in sudden fright. The other horse became frightened also and the carriage started forward in a wild dash around the curve. A satisfied smile spread over Nereus' thin face. In another moment they would reach the spot and that pin would surely split as they turned the curve. There was a crash, a splintering of wood, a girl's frightened cry. Nereus leaned over and took a cautious peep.

He swore in disappointed rage.

The wheel had come off the carriage as he had hoped

it would but he had not counted on the skill of the slave nor on the horses themselves. At the animals' sudden start the slave had pulled them in, at the same time calling to them in soothing tones. The horses were well trained and tender-mouthed, and as the wheel came off and the carriage pitched forward they came to a stop. Another foot or two and the carriage would have been hurtled to the valley below.

Mara and Rachel left the carriage and stood looking down the rocky slope while the slave held the horses and stared ruefully at the broken carriage wheel.

"That was a narrow escape," gasped Rachel through pale lips. "God was surely with us or we would both have been killed."

Mara shrugged. "We were just lucky."

Nereus scrambled over the hill to his waiting horse, cursing what he considered his ill luck but more determined than ever not to abandon what he had set out to do.

Since their first reference to the subject Rachel had said nothing more to Mara about the Baptist, but she had heard of him from others. His name was on the lips of many. The age-long hope of the promised Messiah was living anew in many hearts and the flame of it burned more brightly than ever. There was a breathless expectancy, a constant hope that grew as the days passed. God's promise would not fail and if ever Israel needed a Deliverer, it was now in this, the darkest hour of her degradation. As Rachel had said, many believed that the Baptist was the Messiah, though he had denied that he was. Wherever he appeared, people from every walk of life gathered in crowds to hear him. He had returned to Judea and Rachel was eager to hear him but hesitated to mention her desire to Mara. One day Mara mentioned him herself.

"What does this Baptist look like?" she asked.

"He has a rather stern face though his eyes are kind. He is very much tanned from his life in the wilderness. He's a Nazarite, so his hair and beard are long. He wears a coat of camel's skin." She wondered at Mara's sudden interest in him.

"Does he have any followers who travel with him?"

"Yes, there are quite a number who go with him wherever he goes."

"Let's go and hear him," Mara suggested.

"All right. I've been wanting to hear him again."

The Baptist was already preaching when they arrived. He stood on a small knoll and the people were grouped about, some seated and some standing on the gently sloping, shaded banks of the stream. Mara needed only a glance to tell her that he was the same man she had seen that day on the Joppa Road. As she took her place in the crowd, she sought for the young disciple, but she did not see him. Soon she forgot everything but what the Baptist was saying.

His words swept over them like a lash, sparing no one. He attacked the social and religious life of his people and told them truths that no other since the prophets had dared to speak. He condemned the morals of the men, scoring them for following the example of the nations about them by yielding to the customs that had become common practice among them. He turned his attention to the women and rebuked them for occupying a place in a man's household which was a shame to them and an insult to every true wife.

As Mara listened she felt that every eye must be upon her for it seemed as if he were talking directly to her.

Suddenly he turned to a group of Pharisees who had drawn to one side, apart from the others, and were evidently in entire accord with everything he said.

"O generation of vipers!" he cried, pointing to them, "who hath warned you to flee from the wrath to come?"

Then he launched an attack upon the self-righteousness of the Pharisees. The crowd gasped in amazement. Never had anyone dared to speak such words to these men who held not only the authority of the religious law but had usurped the power of the civil also, assuming, as members of the Sanhedrin, the power of life and death, a power that was upheld in most instances by Rome.

When the Baptist had finished, Mara wondered whether these men would seek to attack him or whether they would turn their backs upon him in silent disdain. She was astonished when one of them spoke in a voice strangely meek.

"What shall we do to meet with your approval?"

Swift and sure came the answer. "Bring forth therefore fruits worthy of repentance, and begin not to say within yourselves, 'We have Abraham to our father,' for I say unto you that God is able of these stones to raise up children unto Abraham. And now also the ax is laid unto the root of the trees: every tree therefore which bringeth not forth good fruit is hewn down, and cast into the fire."

When he had finished his sermon several others from the crowd asked questions. For each he had a ready answer that fitted the question and which offered the means for a better life. A call was made for those who wished to be baptized. The crowd gathered at the water's edge.

Mara's heart was strangely stirred. Her attention was attracted by one of the candidates for baptism. There was something different about him that seemed to set him apart from the others, yet she couldn't understand what it was. He was not tall and there was nothing of the athlete about him, yet he possessed a commanding majesty. His face was not handsome, yet there was something about it more attractive than mere physical beauty. Then she knew what it was that made him seem so different. It was his eyes. There was something in them that baffled and bewildered her.

Suddenly she was conscious that he was looking at her. He did not seem to see her face, but appeared to be looking into her very soul. She felt somehow that he was reading her thoughts, that he could see deep into her heart, that he knew what she was; and the knowledge overwhelmed her with shame.

The Baptist turned and spoke to him in low tones and Mara longed to know what he said, but she couldn't hear above the noisy murmur of the throng. Finally the stranger entered the water and was baptized. As he rose from the water a dove fluttered down and lighted on his shoulder, then flew away again, straight toward the sunlit sky. A deep rumbling like the rolling of distant thunder smote the air.

"I hope it isn't going to rain," Rachel remarked as she looked at the sky. "That's funny. There isn't a cloud anywhere."

Mara didn't answer, for the stranger had come up out of the river and was passing near her. She watched him with fascinated gaze as he approached. As he passed her he looked at her again. She shrank from his gaze and as he disappeared in the crowd a sob struggled in her throat and tears came to her eyes.

"Did you see that man, Rachel?" she asked.

"What man?" asked Rachel, surprised at Mara's agitation.

"The one the dove lighted on. He just passed over there."

"I didn't see him. I was watching that group of Pharisees."

Mara turned to see the Pharisees Rachel was watching. She wondered why she had been so upset and she wished she could forget those searching eyes and the turmoil their glance had caused. As the group she was watching parted, she looked into the eyes of the boy she had met outside the city gate.

She stared at him breathlessly while joy quickened her pulse. She saw him turn and ask a question of someone near him and the man questioned turned and looked at her, then shook his head.

He's trying to find out who I am, she thought. Then the sudden sickening knowledge of who and what she was swept over her. She turned to Rachel.

"Let's go. It's getting late," she said in dull tones of dejection.

Silently they left the throng and Mara sternly refused to allow herself one backward glance, though she knew the stranger was looking eagerly after her.

Chapter Seven

The Unexpected Guest

FOLLOWING HER EXPERIENCE AT THE BANKS OF THE Jordan, Mara was restless and unhappy. Vague regrets and longings dispelled the peace that had come to her before she had heard the Baptist preach. She thought many times of the stranger who had been baptized and had disturbed her so with his soul-seeing, penetrating gaze, and she wondered who he was. She had asked Rachel's friends about him but no one seemed to have noticed him or the dove which lighted on him. Memory of him still disturbed her strangely.

Many times the memory of another pair of eyes and their frank admiration stirred her pulse to quicker beating and wakened a passionate longing to be free.

She made a determined effort to forget these disquieting thoughts and grasped eagerly at anything which promised to take her mind off herself. Rachel sensed her unhappiness and did her utmost to keep her entertained. One afternoon they went for a drive over the mountain road that led to the north. Rachel chattered brightly, striving to distract Mara, for her depression was apparent.

A beautiful panorama spread itself before them. The roadside and the fields beyond were dotted with brilliant-hued poppies and crimson anemones. In the distance the rugged mountain peaks towered higher and higher across the dim blue horizon. The air was heavy with the scent of resin, lemon, geranium and myrrh.

As Mara and Rachel rounded a curve they saw two travelers who seemed to be resting by the roadside. When the sisters drew nearer they discovered that one of the men was stretched upon the ground with his head on his companion's knee. His companion, an old man, signaled to them as they approached. Rachel called to the slave to stop the horses.

As Rachel got out of the carriage Mara caught her breath with a smothered exclamation. The younger man was the one she had met on the Joppa Road.

"What's the matter?" asked Rachel solicitously.

"The boy has a fever," he told her. "We were on our way to the city but he can't go any farther. My name is Simeon. His is Judah. We're followers of the Baptist. I came on business for the Baptist and Judah insisted on coming with me. I didn't know he was sick when we started."

"Have you any relatives in the city?" asked Rachel.

"No. And neither has he. His people are all dead. I'll have to get him to a doctor somehow," he finished helplessly.

"Rachel, take him home with us," Mara whispered.

"Of course I shall. Do you think I'd leave one of the Baptist's followers here on the roadside like this?" She turned back to Simeon and said, "If you'll accept the hospitality of my home, both of you shall be welcome."

Simeon accepted her offer eagerly and gratefully and with the help of the slave he put Judah in the carriage. Mara sat silent as they drove homeward, listening to Rachel's conversation with Simeon. Her eyes were fastened upon the unconscious Judah. How strange it was that he should have come like this when she had been trying so hard to forget him!

Rachel had Judah carried to the guest room upon the roof. She sent for the doctor while Mara, a self-appointed nurse, arranged the pillows beneath his head and bathed his face with cool water. Simeon hovered near, his weather-beaten face grave with anxiety. Judah was sunk in a stupor from which their various ministrations failed to arouse him.

When the doctor came he pronounced the case a serious one.

"It will require careful nursing and constant watching," he informed them. "Only a strong constitution can win the fight. He's been sick too long without attention. Exposure and fatigue have sapped his strength."

"He has a strong constitution, if that's what he needs," Simeon informed the doctor eagerly. "As for the nursing, I'll do my best, but I'm a poor hand in the sickroom."

"Hannah and I will do the nursing," Mara told him. "Hannah's a wonderful nurse."

"The Lord bless you for your kindness," exclaimed Simeon gratefully.

Rachel had been too much occupied with preparations for the patient's comfort to notice Mara's face or she would have been puzzled by its expression. Hannah had seen, however, and understood, for she had recognized Judah. A vague uneasiness possessed her.

Days passed while the fever raged and the stricken boy fought desperately for life. A couch had been put in the room and Hannah was with him constantly. Mara flitted in and out at frequent intervals. Some inner voice warned her that there was danger for her in that room, danger to the hope of happiness she had established so determinedly within her heart. But she couldn't stay away. That face upon the pillow, strong and handsome even in illness, drew her like a loadstone.

Judah seemed to grow steadily worse. Mara insisted upon taking her turn at nursing him. There was little that anyone could do but sit and watch and hope. As hope grew fainter, the thing which Hannah had already seen came as a sudden revelation to Mara.

It left her stunned and rather frightened when she realized that she loved Judah. It seemed so impossible, so fantastic. Yet it was only too true.

One morning the doctor announced that the end was near at hand.

"If the fever isn't broken within the next twenty-four hours, he'll die. He can't go on like this."

All through the long day Mara sat by the bed or walked restlessly up and down on the roof outside. When night came Hannah urged her to take some rest.

"No. I'll stay here tonight, Hannah," she insisted. "You need the rest yourself. Go downstairs to bed."

Reluctantly Hannah obeyed. Simeon hovered near like a wistful child until Mara persuaded him to go to bed, promising to call him if any change took place.

At last she was alone with Judah. For a long time she sat by his side and gazed upon his pale face. He lay so still she could scarcely see him breathe. She put out her hand and touched his as it lay upon the cover. The touch thrilled her. Impulsively she took his hand in both her own and held it against her cheek which was suddenly moist with tears. She knelt by the bed and stroked his fevered cheek gently. She gave voice to her thoughts, scarcely realizing that she was speaking aloud.

"I love you! I love you! I don't know why I do and I know I shouldn't, but I do! It's so wonderful—and so silly—and so terrible! I never knew that love could make anyone suffer like this. Why couldn't I have met you a long time ago? We could have been so happy! Now you're slipping away from me and I shall be so alone all the rest of my life—so—alone—"

Mara put her arm across his breast and laid her head on the pillow with her cheek close to his. She was lost for a while in a world of dreams, but terror seized her and brought her back to reality as a sudden tremor shook him and stopped the regular faint breathing for a moment. The girl raised her head and stared at him with wide, frightened eyes until at last his breathing became regular once more. A sigh of relief escaped her. Impulsively she bent and kissed him on the lips, tremblingly, timidly. Tears ran down her face and sobs shook her as she knelt there watching him.

Rachel had slipped to the doorway to look at Judah. She stood for a moment, petrified by what she saw. Then she went to Mara and put her arm around her.

"My dear! My dear!" she murmured soothingly. "Don't cry like that!"

"I thought you were asleep," Mara stammered.

"I was up with Joseph and I thought I'd come and see how Judah was. I—I—couldn't help seeing," she said.

"It doesn't help any to have you know what I did," Mara admitted.

"I'm sorry," Rachel murmured helplessly. "I never dreamed you'd fall in love with him. It seems too impossible."

"Yes, it does, but it's true. I think I fell in love with him that day on the Joppa Road. He's the boy I told you about," she added, smiling a little at Rachel's astonished stare.

"How strange!" Rachel murmured. Then, putting an arm around Mara, she tried to comfort her. "Don't cry, dear. I have a feeling that he'll get well."

"That won't change things for me. If he knew the truth about me, he'd despise me," Mara replied brokenly.

"Come on downstairs with me and let's send Hannah to take your place," Rachel urged. "You're worn out."

"No. Please! I want to stay here. It may be for only a little while. Then—everything—will be over—for—me."

Silently and understandingly Rachel kissed Mara and left her.

Chapter Eight

A Dream Come True

MARA WAS SO LOST IN THE DEPTHS OF HER UTTER wretchedness that she hadn't noticed the change which had taken place in Judah, the almost imperceptible slipping from the deep stupor to quiet sleep which marked the passing of the crisis as the fever subsided.

She became aware at last that he was looking at her and that his eyes were no longer dull with stupor, but that he was staring at her in surprise and unbelief.

"Is it really you or am I still dreaming?" he asked in a weak, quavering voice while his eyes wandered about the room and then returned to her face.

Her heart began a wild pounding. Did he know about that kiss and had he heard what she had said?

"How did I get here?" he asked, not observing her confusion.

"My sister and I found you and Simeon on the roadside. You were very sick and we brought you here. You've been sick a long time."

"I remember when we left the Baptist," he said in a slow, weak voice. "When I learned that he was going farther north and that Simeon was coming here, I insisted upon coming to Jerusalem with him. I never dreamed I'd find you so easily." A smile spread across his pale lips which filled her with a strange delight as she dropped her eyes in confusion before his gaze.

"The doctor said you were not to talk," she cautioned.

"Did he say I couldn't even ask your name? Please! What is it?"

"My name is Mara," she informed him as her eyes again met his.

"Mara." He lingered on the word.

A sudden silence hung between them while his gaze lingered on her face. She felt that his eyes were telling her things which his lips dared not utter. Or was it only her desire which made her imagine it?

"Mara," he repeated softly. "But 'Mara' means 'bitterness.' "

"Yes." The glad thrill left her heart and it seemed cold and heavy. Bitterness! How well it would suit her after this!

"It should be 'Sara'—'princess.' That would suit you better."

She rose abruptly and said hastily, "I must be going and you must try to be quiet until the doctor comes. I shall send my servant to stay with you until morning."

"Please don't go," he begged. "I'm sorry if I said something I shouldn't have said. I didn't mean to offend you."

"You haven't offended me. But I've been sitting here all night and I'm rather tired."

"I'm sorry! You've been so good to me, taking me in and caring for me. How can I ever repay you?"

"By obeying the doctor's orders and going back to

sleep." Mara smiled and then went quickly out into the night without giving him opportunity to reply.

Outside she found Hannah who had slipped upstairs and was asleep under the trellis. Hannah wakened at her touch.

"The fever has left him and he's conscious," Mara told her.

"The Lord be praised!" Hannah exclaimed. "Now he will get well and my poor lamb will be happy again. I'll go in and sit beside him."

Hannah went inside and Mara stood for a moment by the balustrade looking out over the city. The scent of roses and lilies made the air faintly sweet. How beautiful the city looked in the crimson light of the new day! Over the hills the great red sun was peeping, flecking the valley with splashes of gold between the shadows. How peaceful it seemed down there! Would she ever know peace again?

Mara stole softly to Judah's window and stood looking at him as he slept. A struggle began in her heart between the longing to snatch at one brief interval of happiness and the fear of the tragedy which might follow if she yielded to her desire. Why couldn't she be happy for a little while and then slip out of his life, never letting him know the truth about herself? Herod would never know and it would mean so much to her in the dreary years to come—and they would be dreary now indeed. Finally, in utter weariness, she went to her room and tried in vain to sleep. Late in the afternoon Rachel came in with a cup of hot milk.

"How is Judah?" Mara asked as she sipped the milk.

"The doctor thinks he will get well now if he's careful not to overtax his strength. You'd better go and see him for a little while. He's been asking for you."

"I'm not going to see him any more," Mara replied dully.

"Why not?" Rachel asked, and then realized how stupid her question was.

"I don't think I should. It would only make me more unhappy than I am."

"All right, dear, if that's the way you feel about it, but I don't know what excuse I can give to Judah. What shall I tell him?"

"Oh, I don't know! I don't know!" Mara cried brokenly. "Rachel, what should I do? Tell me! If it were Samuel up there, what would you do, if you were—I?"

"I'd go to him," Rachel said emphatically.

"Even if you knew that nothing but suffering and longing would follow you the rest of your life?" Mara persisted.

"Yes, because I should have this little time to remember and it would help me to bear the loneliness and the longing."

"But you know that Samuel loves you." A note of wistfulness crept into Mara's voice.

Rachel smiled though there were tears in her eyes. "If you could have heard the thousand questions Judah asked Hannah about you, you'd know he's at least a little bit interested in you."

"Then you advise me to go?" Mara asked eagerly.

"No, child," Rachel cried, half afraid of the effect of her words. "I wouldn't advise you. That's something you must decide for yourself."

"O Rachel, it isn't fair! It isn't fair!" Mara moaned. "Why can't I have the chance to be happy? Why is there no way out for me?"

"You closed the way yourself, Mara," Rachel said tactlessly as tears filled her eyes.

"This isn't a time to reproach me, Rachel!" Mara cried brokenly.

"I didn't mean to reproach you, dear." Rachel stroked Mara's tumbled mass of hair. "How I wish I could help you!"

Mara was silent for a while, struggling against the call of her heart, fighting again the battle between desire and her own better judgment. Finally she got up and went to the chest where she kept her clothes. There was a reckless light in her eyes as she began to dress.

"I'm going to him," she declared. "Why shouldn't I? I don't care what happens! I didn't seek him. I tried to forget him. If fate brought him here, then fate can take care of us both."

"What if Herod should find out?" asked Rachel, suddenly afraid.

"He'd kill me, I suppose." Mara shrugged her shoulders. "But I won't worry about that now. Perhaps when this is over I'll be glad if he does kill me."

She put on a dull blue robe with a girdle of silver. Carefully she combed her long fair hair and fastened a fillet of pearls across her forehead. When the task was finished she surveyed herself in the long mirror of polished metal, then turned to Rachel for her inspection.

"Will I do?" she asked with forced gaiety.

"You're beautiful," was Rachel's comment.

Mara kissed her lightly, waved gaily to her and left her. She slipped into Judah's room and stood beside the bed. He seemed to be asleep but presently he opened his eyes and lay looking at her. The dying sun touched her hair and illumined her face with a mellow glow, giving it an ethereal quality that emphasized its beauty.

"I hope you're feeling better," she said primly as she seated herself.

"Much better, thank you. The doctor said I could talk, and I'm afraid I wore Hannah out."

"She didn't look tired." Mara smiled. "She looked as if she had been enjoying herself."

"I'm sure she was because we were talking about you. I've discovered that Hannah loves to talk about you."

"Perhaps I'd better ask the doctor to give orders to Hannah not to talk so much."

"I asked Hannah a question that she didn't answer." His eyes searched her face. "She said I'd better ask you."

"I don't promise to answer it either." Her heart began to beat faster as she met his gaze.

"May I ask it anyway?" he begged.

"Yes, of course."

"Do you remember meeting me one afternoon on the Joppa Road?"

She caught her breath as he smiled.

"I thought you were the most beautiful girl I had ever seen and I stood there staring at you like a dunce. After you had passed me, I turned back to get a last look at you."

There was a twinkle in his eye and suddenly they both laughed.

"I was hoping you'd remember," he said. "Blessings certainly do come in disguise at times. I was so upset when I felt my strength giving out on the way back here to Jerusalem. How silly I was to worry!"

"That journey almost caused your death," she reminded him.

"Yes, but just look what it brought me! I found you again. I told Hannah all about why I wanted to come back here when the Baptist was going back into Galilee."

"You must have told Hannah a great many things."

"I did. I told her things I wouldn't dare tell you—yet—for fear you'd think I was taking advantage of your hospitality."

Simeon came in just then and, glad of an excuse, Mara told Judah good night and left him.

During the days that followed, in the brief intervals they were together she adroitly kept the conversation from becoming too personal. She longed to hear him say the words which she felt he was impatient to utter, yet she was afraid.

"I'm getting well so fast that I'll soon be out of bed," he remarked one evening. "Then it won't be long before I'll have to leave."

"We—shall—miss you," she said, trying to keep the tremor from her voice. She realized suddenly and overwhelmingly what it would mean to her when he did finally leave her. The loneliness, the emptiness and the weight of the knowledge seemed more than she could bear.

"Will you miss me—really?" he asked, and there was no mistaking the look in his eyes.

"Of course I shall."

He put out his hand and took hers as it rested on the side of the bed and words tumbled from his lips as if he had held them captive and could no longer restrain them. "You must have known all along that I love you, Mara. I've told you every time I looked at you, from the first moment I opened my eyes and saw you here by the bed. I've loved you ever since that day on the Joppa Road. It was the hope of finding you and of knowing you that brought me here with Simeon. Am I foolish to hope that you care a little?" His hand tightened its hold on hers.

The time was too short and this joy would be too brief for her to pretend coyness or diffidence. She knew she must take advantage of every precious moment and drain it of all its joy, for soon he would be gone and only emptiness and longing would remain.

"You must have known all along that I cared," she murmured.

"I've dreamed of you every night since that first meeting," he continued, drawing her closer, "and one night after I came here I dreamed that you knelt by the bed and kissed me. Somehow that kiss seemed to draw me back from death and give me a new hold on life."

"Oh, then you knew all along!" she cried. "You weren't asleep!"

"I didn't know. I was just hoping it wasn't a dream, but ever since, I've been hoping that if it was, you'd one day make the dream come true. Kiss me, Mara." He drew her to him, and after a moment's hesitation she slipped to her knees and rested within the circle of his arms, while her lips rested tenderly upon his.

"Oh, the wonder of it," he whispered as he held her to him. "I'll never get over the wonder of it all—my meeting you and finding you so soon—the wonder that you could love me—the wonder of you!"

The wonder of you! The words echoed within her heart, and with them came sudden overwhelming shame as she remembered who and what she was. She withdrew herself from his arms and with a murmured excuse she left him, ashamed to meet his eyes again.

Chapter Nine

Herod Has His Way

HERODIAS WALKED BACK AND FORTH UPON THE MARBLE floor of the room while a frown contracted her heavy brows and there was a discontented droop to her full red lips. Her long black robe glittered with iridescent beaded embroidery, giving a serpentlike appearance to her slow, graceful movements.

Herod watched her moodily from under his bushy brows and the resemblance seemed surprisingly strong to him. She was a snake, he mused, a sinuous, beautiful reptile who had wrapped her coils about him and now held him helpless in her power. But it wouldn't be forever! Soon he would no longer fear to cut those coils and rid himself of what he had once so desperately desired.

"You're silly to want that stupid fellow to preach before you," Herodias remarked.

"Silly or not, I've made up my mind to hear him and I'm not going to change it just to satisfy your whim."

"It isn't to satisfy my whim," she retorted. "Can't you see you're only encouraging him and making these stupid Jews flock to hear him all the more by making them believe that you think he's a great person?"

"Perhaps he is and I might learn a few things from

him. He's great enough to make the Jews flock to hear what he says. They've never been eager to listen to what I had to say."

She knew he was trying to annoy her and the knowledge made her furious.

"You haven't sense enough to see that you're in danger of having him take your throne from you. All these Jews need is a leader to make Roman blood flow again as it did in the days of the Maccabees. And your blood would be the first to flow."

"Nonsense! This fellow's a preacher, not a fighter. You're just peevish because you can't have your own way. You had it about Mara and you ought to be satisfied. But you never will be!"

He stalked heavily from the room. She watched him go and there was a smoldering blaze in her black eyes. It was true. It seemed that nothing would satisfy her. The bitterness of remorse and regret had eaten into her soul and destroyed her capacity for happiness, robbed her of all hope of peace or contentment. Why, oh, why had she left Philip? She had been happy with him, even though he had never stirred her as Herod or Nereus had.

What kind of creature was she, she asked herself wretchedly, torn between such conflicting desires, drawn by such irresistible aspirations when she knew they could not bring happiness? She seemed to be struggling in a stream of crosscurrents, longing for Philip, wanting Herod's love, yet growing to despise him, craving Nereus, reaching out for something which seemed always just beyond her reach, driven by some unseen force beyond her control.

This sudden whim of Herod's to hear John the Baptist angered her and filled her with foreboding. She would be forced to sit with Herod and listen to him or else run the risk of offending the people she hoped to rule. This would only serve to increase the popularity of the Baptist.

Herod went ahead with his plan to hear the Baptist and there was nothing she could do but submit to it. As they took their places on the balcony and waited for the Baptist to begin preaching, she observed the complacent smirk on Herod's face. He was like a child, glorying in his petty victory over her. Her lip curled disdainfully as she gazed over the throng. She was dressed with all the splendor of royalty, in a robe of dull bronze silk with a fillet of gold about her hair and bracelets encircling her arm to the elbow. She was conscious of the admiring glances of those about her as well as their hostility. Only their admiration mattered to her.

She listened with an air of bored indifference as the Baptist began his sermon but her indifference was completely shattered when the preacher boldly denounced Herod for having stolen his brother's wife. Her startled gaze swept over the throng and she heard their murmurs of approval of the preacher's words.

Herod's face went from purple to white and back to purple again as he grasped the full meaning of the Baptist's words. His surprised, half-frightened gaze sought Herodias.

"Have that man arrested at once," she said in low tones.

Herod hesitated a moment, then shook his head and

left the balcony without saying a word. There was nothing left for her to do but to follow.

Inside, she turned upon him furiously. "I hope you're satisfied with the sermon you heard," she blazed.

"I don't know what possessed him to say that," Herod muttered helplessly.

"You gave him the opportunity to say the thing that would appeal to the people and increase his popularity. You did it to show me you would have your own way. You should be happy over the result of your demonstration."

"You should be happy, too!" he flared. "It's given you another chance to use your tongue."

"Are you going to arrest him?" she demanded.

"No, I'm not. If I did that after what's happened, I'd have the people howling about my ears. I'm afraid to arrest him."

"You'll be sorry if you don't," she warned.

"I seem to be sorry for everything I do," he retorted irritably.

Sorry! Yes, they were both sorry but there was nothing they could do but go on. After their goal was reached, what remained?

Chapter Ten

An Interlude

JUDAH'S RECOVERY WAS SLOWER THAN HE HAD ANTICI-
pated. Days passed before he was able to get out of bed.
Rachel and Samuel urged him to stay with them until
he was able to follow the Baptist and he was glad of an
excuse to remain near Mara. Promising to return when
the Baptist left Galilee, Simeon had left as soon as Judah
was out of danger.

It was a trying time for Mara. Her joy at Judah's presence was tempered by the knowledge that the more she
was with him the more terrible the final parting would
be. She would not think of the future, for it filled her
with terror—fear that Herod would discover her unfaithfulness to him; a greater fear that Judah would find out
the truth; an ever-present dread that Herod would cut
short this stolen interval of joy by sending for her before
Judah left.

Hannah hovered near them, a silent sentinel sitting
near the balustrade. She watched Mara with a heavy
heart, knowing the danger and realizing how short-
lived this interlude must be.

Rachel went about her various duties with a fixed

smile. She knew the inevitable end of this stolen romance and fear smote her when she thought of what would happen should it be discovered. The punishment for an unfaithful concubine was a terrible death.

At length Simeon returned and reported that the Baptist was again on his way to Jerusalem.

"Do you think you'll be able to join us, lad?" he asked.

"Yes, I think so," Judah told him but there was a strange lack of enthusiasm in his voice.

"I'm afraid the Baptist has gotten himself into trouble," Simeon informed him, "and we're all worried over it but he doesn't seem to be."

"What's happened?" asked Judah anxiously.

"While we were in Galilee, Herod sent for him to preach to him. The Baptist denounced Herod for having stolen Herodias from Philip."

"Why did he do that?" asked Mara.

"I don't know, unless it was the sight of that woman decked out like a queen, with that scornful smile on her lips. She was furious and tried to make Herod arrest him, but Herod was afraid to do it because the Baptist was surrounded by a crowd and they all approved of what he had said. That made her more furious."

"He'd better be careful," Mara warned. "Herodias won't stop at anything and she'll hate him for this."

"The Baptist isn't afraid of Herodias," Simeon told her. "He said the other day, 'My task is finished. There is one coming who is mightier than I. He must increase but I must decrease.'"

"What did he mean by that?" asked Mara. She wished Simeon would leave her alone with Judah now that the time was so short.

"He means that the Messiah will soon be here."

"Does anyone really believe that?" she asked.

They both stared at her in surprise; then Simeon remarked, "That's a strange way for a daughter of Abraham to speak."

"I mean that people have been looking for him so long that it just doesn't seem as if he's ever coming," she amended lamely, frightened at the slip she had made.

"The Baptist says the time is at hand. But even if he hadn't said that, we would still be looking for him. Since that rumor over thirty years ago that a king had been born in Bethlehem, the hearts of our people have been stirred to a greater hope. It's a wonder your sister has ever let that hope die within your heart."

"Oh, she hasn't! But I get so impatient for us to be free from Roman rule."

"What made the Baptist say that the time is at hand?" asked Judah. "Has anything happened since I left him?"

"Something happened some time ago at the Jordan, though the Baptist didn't mention it then. It seems that he baptized someone and a dove lighted on that person. Then a voice spoke to the Baptist from heaven and told him that this man was the Messiah."

"Oh, I saw that!" cried Mara excitedly. "I asked so many about it but nobody seemed to have seen it."

"If you saw that, then you saw the Messiah," Simeon informed her in reverent tones.

Mara stared at him with wide eyes, remembering that scene at the Jordan, those soul-seeing eyes of the stranger and the unrest and shame which filled her heart as a result. But she put that scene and its memories from her with a determined effort. She would not think of anything but Judah and these last few hours with him!

Late that evening she and Judah were alone on the roof. He was to leave with Simeon the following morning. Mara knew this would be their last hour together and her heart was heavy.

"I want to tell Simeon about us," Judah said as he put his arm about her and drew her to him.

"Why does he have to know?" she cried in panic.

"He'd have to know if we were married, wouldn't he?"

"We're not even betrothed yet," she evaded.

"We can be, before I leave. We can go this evening and have our betrothal ceremony performed. It will take so long for that year to pass." His lips touched her cheek; then he swept her to him and kissed her.

She felt the beating of his heart and her own leaped in quick response until she remembered and the gladness vanished suddenly.

"We can't go tonight," she said heavily.

"Why not?"

"I—I—don't think Rachel and Samuel would consent," she faltered. "I'd rather wait until you come back again. And, please, wait until we're betrothed before you say anything about our being in love."

"What's the matter, Mara?" he asked, noticing her agitation, while his arms loosened their hold about her.

"Nothing. You're not angry, are you?" she cried in alarm.

"No, I'm not angry." But his voice betrayed hurt and disappointment. "I can't blame you for hesitating to marry me. I haven't anything worthy of you to offer you now. But it won't always be this way, I promise you. Some day I'll be able to give you all that you've been used to."

"Oh, it isn't that, Judah!" she exclaimed as she nestled against him. "You're all I want! I'm not caring about whether you have much or little. I love you! Nothing else matters!"

"Then why are you afraid for anyone to know we love each other?" he persisted.

"I'm not afraid. I'd just rather wait until you come back. I'm sure Rachel would rather we waited. Can't you do that?"

"I'll have to," he admitted.

"Will you be away very long?"

"I don't know."

Rachel joined them then and Mara was glad for the interruption.

Early the next morning Judah left. In his eyes there was disappointment and a faint reproach which she pretended not to see. She smiled gaily as they left and waved to them from the housetop. Tears dimmed her eyes so that she could scarcely see them as they passed down the narrow street and out of sight around the corner.

Chapter Eleven

A Broken Promise

SHADOWS WERE GATHERING ON THE DISTANT MOUNTAIN slopes while Mara sat on the roof looking over the city and thinking of Judah and their last time together. Within the houses along the narrow street there was the clatter of pots and pans and the voices of children came to her through the open windows near by.

Rachel had gone for a visit in the neighborhood and had invited Mara to go with her, but Mara had begged to be excused from going. She felt too restless and miserable to join in the light chatter of friendly neighbors. As the time approached when she could reasonably expect Judah to return, her unhappiness increased. She was eager to see him again; yet she dreaded the meeting and the renewal of the question of their betrothal ceremony.

She almost wished that Herod would send for her before Judah came back. The thought of going back to Galilee, however, filled her with dismay. How could she ever return to the life she had lived and again pretend a love she didn't feel? Wouldn't Herod guess the truth? The memory of Herod's caresses filled her with loathing. What a tangled web her life had become! It seemed that ahead of her lay nothing but longing and emptiness and the bitterness of regret.

"I have good news for you," Rachel announced as she came up the steps and roused Mara from her unhappy reverie. "The Baptist has returned."

"Then Judah will be here soon!" Mara cried as joy swept over her. Forgotten were her gloomy thoughts and regrets and fears. Soon she would be with him again. Nothing else mattered.

"The Baptist was preaching this afternoon just outside the city," Rachel continued. "Everybody seems terribly excited over his return. He preaches a different message now from what he preached before. He says that the Messiah is at hand and that he will soon appear."

"Did you get excited over that news?" asked Mara indifferently.

"Of course I did. Why shouldn't I? Think of what it will mean to have a king of the Jews reigning here in Jerusalem! Haven't you ever thought of the possibilities of such a thing, Mara?"

There was a sob in Mara's voice as she replied. She was talking to herself more than to Rachel.

"Yes, I've thought about what it would mean to have a king reigning here in Jerusalem. The thought thrilled me once. But it doesn't any more. Kings and thrones don't mean anything to me any more."

Rachel misunderstood her but hastened to change the subject.

"What are you going to do about Judah?" she asked. "You can't keep putting him off and you know that when he returns he's going to want to ask Samuel's consent for the betrothal ceremony to be performed. You'll have to tell him sooner or later that you can't marry him."

"No! I'll never do that. I'll never tell him. I couldn't bear it if he knew the truth about me!"

"But he will find out sometime," Rachel told her.

"Yes, I suppose he will," Mara admitted. "But if he finds out after I've gone, I won't be near him to see the scorn in his eyes. I'll be where I can never see him again. Nothing will matter then."

"I'm afraid you've been forgetting Judah, my dear. Have you been quite fair to him, leading him to hope when you knew there was no hope for him?" Rachel chided her gently.

"I did forget how he would feel!" cried Mara. "I was only thinking of myself. Oh, why did you remind me of it? It makes it so much harder for me to bear, remembering this."

"I'm sorry, Mara darling. Forgive me. How I wish I could do something to make it easier for you both!"

A knock at the outer door broke into their conversation and a few moments later they heard Judah's voice below. Mara turned eager eyes toward the stairway, forgetting everything but that sound of his voice while Rachel slipped away unobserved. He came toward her with outstretched arms and with a glad little cry she went to him.

As her eyes traveled lingeringly over his tanned face, so ruggedly handsome, she realized how much she had feared she would never see him again.

He held her at arm's length while he looked at her intently. "If I were a poet," he began, "perhaps I could tell you how beautiful you are. What was it Solomon said? 'Thy lips are like a thread of scarlet.' That doesn't begin to say how lovely your mouth is, with that little dimple just beneath, in your chin."

A low laugh of sheer joy rippled from her lips. "Doesn't Solomon's poem say that her eyes were like two fish pools? Don't you dare call my eyes fish pools! I'd feel all slimy and scaly."

"I'd say they were like two amber gems, fit only to adorn er—well—er—the crown of the queen of Sheba." He finished lamely, laughing.

"I don't think you'll do as a poet. The next thing I know you'll be telling me my skin is like the queen of Sheba's. If I'm not mistaken, hers was black."

"Perhaps I'd better stick to Solomon." He smiled as he drew her to him again. "You're like a pure 'lily among thorns.' Solomon must have been thinking of someone like you when he wrote that," he added tenderly.

Her joy vanished as a sob rose in her throat and seemed about to choke her as she struggled to keep from crying aloud. A pure lily!

He didn't observe her agitation as he seated himself and drew her down beside him. "There's so much I want to tell you," he began, "and I have so little time. The Baptist is going back to Galilee and we leave at daybreak tomorrow."

"He shouldn't go back to Galilee if he's made Herodias so furious. She'll be sure to take revenge upon him in some way," Mara interrupted.

"That's what we've tried to make him believe. We've tried to persuade him not to go, but some inner force seems to be driving him on. He says he must preach again in Galilee and prepare the way for the Messiah. He says we may expect him any day, to declare himself."

"Do you really think he'll ever come, Judah?"

"I believe that in less than a year he'll be ruling here in Jerusalem," he said in eager, fervent tones.

The possibilities of such a situation thrilled her with a new hope and she exclaimed, "It sounds too good to be true!" Then, after a moment, she added, "If he should come and rule, even Herod's slaves would be free, wouldn't they?"

"Of course they would. Herod will be lucky if he escapes with his life."

Like a cold shower, washing away all the joy of this new hope, came the memory of what she was. "What good would it do to be free?" she murmured, forgetting herself.

"What do you mean?" he asked, puzzled by the look on her face. It was pale and drawn in the dim light.

She recovered herself with an effort. "I was thinking of those poor creatures he's made his concubines. Even if the Messiah should free them, they would always be outcasts. Even the Messiah could do nothing for them."

"Let's not worry about Herod's slaves. We have other things more important to talk about. I did something before I came here that I hope you'll approve of."

His air of suppressed excitement roused her curiosity. "What did you do?" she asked.

"I made arrangements with the rabbi for our betrothal. I told him I was leaving town and he agreed to perform the ceremony tonight."

"Why did you do that?" she cried. "You've never even asked Samuel if you could."

"The answer is very simple," he replied, laughing. "I want to marry you. If we're not betrothed, we'll never be married. If the year of betrothal never begins, it will never end. And I still have time to ask Samuel. He'll be willing if you are, I'm sure."

"I can't go tonight," she answered in a strained voice as she rose and turned from him to hide her agitation.

He followed her and turned her so that he could look into her face. "Why not?" he wanted to know. "You promised we could be betrothed the next time I came. What's happened? Have you changed your mind about loving me?"

"No! No!" She clung to him desperately. "I could never change my mind about loving you! I shall always love you, Judah, no matter what happens."

"Then why are you so unwilling for us to be betrothed?"

She couldn't meet his probing eyes. Her gaze wandered to the stairway. Her eyes dilated with sudden horror and she stood transfixed at what she saw. Just slipping out of sight was the head of a man. In the dim light she couldn't be sure, but the features were remarkably like those of Nereus. She broke away from Judah with a frightened cry.

"What's the matter?" he asked in alarm.

"There was someone peeping at us over the balustrade. I saw him right there by the stairway!"

"Don't be frightened," he soothed. "It was only some inquisitive passer-by. What difference does it make if he did see us?"

"But that face! That face!"

"Who was it?" he asked in surprise.

"Oh—I—I—don't know," she stammered. "But he looked so vicious that he frightened me."

He gained possession of her hands and drew her to him. "Don't be afraid. No one can hurt you. Besides, he's gone. Let's forget him. We have something more important to talk about. Have you forgotten?"

"No," she answered in calmer tones, "but we can't be betrothed just now, Judah. Really we can't. I—I'm sorry."

"But it may be months before I come back, Mara. You put me off before without any real excuse. Now you're doing the same thing again. There must be some reason. Surely I have a right to know, unless you've decided you don't want to marry me."

His voice was cold with disappointment and a faint doubt.

"Please don't think that!" she begged. "That's not the reason. I do want to marry you! Be patient just a little while longer and when you come back I'll be willing. I promise you."

"That's what you said before."

"I know. But this time I'll keep my promise."

"Is there someone else?" he asked with sudden suspicion.

She grasped recklessly at the excuse that would be a way out. "Yes. There is—is—a man Samuel wants me to marry. He—he's been very insistent about it and—and—things haven't been so pleasant since I refused to listen to him. For Rachel's sake I promised to wait until—until she can make Samuel see things our way. Won't you be patient and wait a little while longer?"

She wondered what her good-natured, indulgent brother-in-law would think if he heard this lie.

"I'll have to," he admitted. "But you won't let him talk you into marrying this man, will you?" he asked anxiously.

"Never! Never! He couldn't make me do that! Please don't be angry with me, Judah. I couldn't bear it to have you leave me angry."

He kissed her and assured her that he wasn't angry, but his disappointment and hurt hung over them like a cloud and before long he had to leave her. As she listened to his footsteps grow fainter in the distance, they seemed to beat time to the throbbing ache in her heart.

Chapter Twelve

A Bargain Is Suggested

THE RIFT BETWEEN HEROD AND HERODIAS HAD WIDENED still more since the Baptist's denunciation of the ruler. Though Herod realized he had gotten himself into this uncomfortable situation, the knowledge only made him more peevish and irritable toward his wife than ever. He felt that Herodias was secretly laughing at him because of the result of his attempt to assert his authority over her.

She knew that he feared and distrusted her and she realized it was largely because of the threats she had so foolishly made when they had quarreled over Mara. She wondered if she had done right in forcing him to send her away. Too late she saw that Mara's absence only made him want her more. What a fool she had been! She could have disposed of the girl without letting Herod know that she had discovered his infatuation. No, regardless of how the girl met her death, he would always suspect that her hand was in it.

He had not missed Nereus from the palace until after the episode of the Baptist. She was glad of that, for now she had a plausible excuse for his absence. As she had known he would, he finally asked her where Nereus was.

"I sent him to follow the Baptist," she explained glibly.

"What for?" he demanded petulantly, sensing some new scheme.

"That's a stupid question. To see whether or not he's trying to stir up the people against you."

"That should be my business, not yours," he informed her.

"It should be but you didn't attend to it. I'm not willing to take any chances of having all our plans upset by that fellow."

"Getting afraid of your own shadow?" he taunted.

"Perhaps. But it's better to be afraid of shadows and find they're only shadows than to have realities come when it's too late to do anything about them."

As time passed and Nereus did not return, Herodias' impatience grew and with it came fear that he would not succeed or that he would bungle the job. He returned at last, however, and sought an interview with her.

Her smoldering eyes glowed with unwilling admiration as she surveyed the keen dark face with the thick hair brushed smoothly back from the broad, high forehead. There was the look of the conqueror about Nereus, the air of one who is always sure of himself. If he were in Herod's place, what a king he would be! She was nearer to loving him then than she had ever been.

"What have you to report?" she asked eagerly.

"Much," he replied. "I've discovered something that will please you better than the girl's death."

"Do you mean to say that you came away from Jerusalem after all this time and left that girl alive?" she demanded as a spark of anger flashed in her eyes.

"Have patience, please! Wait until I finish and then you'll agree with me that we're both very fortunate that I didn't carry out your orders even though I tried to do so. Mara has a sweetheart. And she's desperately in love with the fellow."

"A sweetheart!" Herodias exclaimed as the anger died from her eyes and a strange light dawned there.

"Yes, and what's even more important, this fellow is a follower of John the Baptist. I looked in on a very touching love scene one evening, after I had dogged the girl's footsteps and spied on her for days, trying to find some way in which to dispose of her without also disposing of my own neck. Does this discovery open up any possibilities to you?"

"You're a clever man, Nereus. How lucky I am to have your fidelity!" She put her hand upon his as it lay upon his knee. "I won't forget it, I promise you."

His hand closed over hers as he said, "It's not fidelity that you have from me, my dear, but my love. You know that, but don't ever forget it."

At the touch of his hand there was a quickening of her heart beat and an added tinge of color came into her face.

"Why do you bring that up at the most inopportune times?" she asked with a pout. "Herod is growing very suspicious of me lately. What if he should suspect the truth about you?"

"Sometimes I wish he would. Then perhaps he'd throw you out and you'd be glad to come to me."

"Don't be a fool, Nereus," she exclaimed as she withdrew her hand impatiently. "He'd more likely have you crucified. Do you think I'd be glad to come to anyone who had caused me to lose a throne? Tell me how you found out about Mara and this fellow."

"I played eavesdropper on the outer stairway whenever I got the chance. This boy, Judah, was there in Rachel's home, ill. For a long time Mara didn't leave the house and that old servant Hannah guarded the roof like a grim watchdog. She seemed to sense that some danger threatened Mara. I couldn't find out what was going on. At last I managed to get up the stairs and I saw this touching love scene. Judah was begging Mara to have their betrothal ceremony performed and she was putting him off without telling him the truth. I almost laughed aloud as I listened. Can you imagine this fellow begging Herod's concubine to marry him? I wondered what would happen if I should suddenly appear and tell him the truth."

There was a brief silence while Nereus watched the play of emotions across her face.

Presently he said, "It may please you to know that the Baptist plans to return to Galilee."

A sudden blaze of fury flashed in her eyes. "If he dares to set foot in Herod's jurisdiction, I'll find a way to punish him if it's the last act of my life! If Herod hadn't been such a coward, he'd have had him beheaded long ago. Of course you know what he said when he was here."

"Yes, I heard about it. The news was all over Judea. I think Herod was wise not to harm the Baptist. It would only have weakened his own cause with the people. They think the Baptist is a great prophet."

"Prophet or no prophet, he won't escape so easily this time!"

"This time you may be able to persuade Herod to have him arrested," he suggested.

"How?" Seeing that he had some plan, she was eager to hear it.

"You might make a bargain with Herod. Offer to let him have Mara return if he will arrest the Baptist. When the Baptist is arrested, this fellow Judah can be arrested at the same time. A meeting can be arranged between the lovers and you can manage to have Herod witness the meeting. I have an idea he'll hear something that will make him forget he ever loved the girl."

"We must have some excuse to arrest this fellow," she objected. "We can't keep him in prison without some charge against him—not just at this time, after all that has happened."

"We can make the excuse to arrest him. I think that can be managed. Down in Jerusalem the people are looking for a king to deliver them from Roman dominion. Judah was telling Mara that the Baptist was preparing the way for this king. Don't you see? It all fits in perfectly. He can be arrested on a charge of treason against Rome. He's young and impetuous enough to put up a fight, if we try to arrest him. If you'll let me handle the arrest, I'll see that he causes trouble. That will give me an excuse to take him with the Baptist.

When Herod finds that he's in love with Mara, then it won't matter what happens to the fellow."

"That's a splendid idea." A pleased smile flashed across Herodias' face.

The curtains parted and Herod's angry voice interrupted them. "What does this mean?" he demanded furiously. "What are you doing here, Nereus? Your duties do not bring you into my wife's apartments."

"He had important business to discuss with me," Herodias replied coldly. Then, turning to Nereus, she said casually, as if no storm of emotions swept over her, "You may go, Nereus."

Nereus bowed himself out without answering Herod while the ruler turned to Herodias with a gleam of jealous rage in his eyes. He was glad for an excuse to give vent to the anger which had been smoldering within him for so long.

"Has it come to the point where I can't ask questions of my own soldiers?" he demanded.

"Of course not. But I didn't want you to make a scene before him. Besides, he belongs to my own personal guard and he's under my orders, by your own command. Why shouldn't I have him come here?"

"I'm beginning to understand why you were so insistent that he should be your own personal guard." A cruel gleam came into his eyes. "I was a fool not to have suspected it long ago when you first brought him here."

Sudden fear sent a chill through her. She spoke far more calmly than she felt. "How silly that is! You know very well why I wanted him here. I needed someone near me I could trust. You realized that and agreed to it. Nereus has proved his faithfulness many times."

"I was a fool not to realize long ago just why he was so faithful," he sputtered, unwilling to be convinced that she spoke the truth.

She strove to quiet the rising fear in her heart. Just how much did he know? Had he heard something or was it all suspicion?

"You'd love to find something against me to get even with me for discovering your own unfaithfulness, wouldn't you?" Her voice was soft and conciliatory.

"You're just trying to evade the answer to my question," he retorted. "You haven't told me what Nereus was doing here. What was this important business he had to discuss with you?"

"He was telling me about the Baptist. I told you he had been following this fellow under my orders. And he's discovered that the Baptist is just what I warned you he was: the head of a rabble that is trying to incite the people to revolt. They're planning to put some Jewish king on the throne at Jerusalem. If he succeeds in doing that, then where will your kingdom be?"

"How do you know this is true?"

"Ask Nereus, if you don't believe me. He says that the Baptist is coming back here to stir up trouble in Galilee. Nereus says that the people down in Jerusalem are in a fever of excitement and that they will likely give Pilate trouble before he's through with them."

Herod paced restlessly up and down the room. "Something like this would have to happen, just when I think things are going along smoothly," he complained. "Why does that fool want to come back here? He ought to thank me for not having him arrested before. The minute he starts trouble I'll put him behind bars."

"Wouldn't it be better to do that before he starts trouble?" Herodias asked with just the right shade of indifference in her voice. "It would be much harder to quiet a mob he had stirred to violence than to arrest him before they even knew he was in Galilee."

He was silent a moment but she could see that he was impressed and her spirits rose. "I don't want to do anything that would turn people against me and make them hate me more than they do," he finally said.

"If the Baptist's inciting the people to revolt, he's an enemy of the Roman government and it's your duty to arrest him. Tiberius would commend such an act."

"That's true. But I'm afraid of this man, Herodias. He has some uncanny power over the people. Arresting him might be the very worst thing I could do."

"Nonsense! Better to arrest him now than to wish later that you had." She put an arm about his shoulder. "Come, my dear, don't look so gloomy. Would it make you any happier if I told you that I'd be willing to let Mara come back?"

He stared at her suspiciously though he brightened perceptibly. "What's made you change your mind about her?" he wanted to know.

"I'm just willing to let bygones be bygones. We can never get anywhere by being at daggers' points with each other as we have been lately. It was silly of me to act as I did about her. I've been thinking about it lately and I see where I was wrong. I know you still care for me, but I was so insanely jealous that I just forgot to be reasonable about Mara."

"I told you you were foolish to get into such a rage over her," he said more cheerfully. "I'm glad you've come to your senses."

"I shall be happier now that I have," she smiled, "for I'm sure you'll be in a better humor."

"If I send for her to come back, don't you dare try any of your tricks on her," he warned, his bluster returning. He felt that he had gained another victory over her and the conviction restored his good humor.

"Still suspicious of me, aren't you?" she chided. "I promise I'll leave her entirely to you. And there'll be no more arguments about her. I promise that, too."

"The gods be praised for that!" he ejaculated, and turned to leave the room. He was on fire with impatience to get the messenger on his way to Mara.

"You'll give the order for the arrest of the Baptist as soon as he enters Galilee, won't you?" she called after him.

"What is this, a bargain or another of your plots?" he asked irritably, pausing at the door.

"Don't be foolish! His arrest concerns you as much as it does me. What difference does it make if it is part of a plot, if it gives you what you want?"

"I suppose I had better arrest him if what you say about him is true," he conceded. "If he's innocent, he can prove it at his trial."

"Nereus says that one of his followers has made personal threats against you. Perhaps you'd better have him arrested with the Baptist. Then it won't look as if you had a personal grudge against the Baptist. Nereus says he can identify this fellow."

"All right. I'll give the order at once." He hurried away before she could stop him again.

As the door closed behind him she sank upon the cushioned divan with a sigh of relief.

Poor fool! A harsh laugh burst from her crimson lips. *How easy it was! Much, much easier than I had thought it would be.*

Chapter Thirteen

The Dance of Hate

EACH YEAR HEROD LOOKED FORWARD WITH THE EAGER
anticipation of a child to the celebration of his birthday. He usually gave a great feast to which he invited
not only his own court officials but people of rank or
importance from the other provinces. He sought to make
it the one great event of the year and spared no ex-
travagance or effort to accomplish his desire.

He sent to the Far East for rare and costly foods,
ordered wine in vast quantities, imported the best entertainers his scouts could assemble. The event was an
orgy of feasting and drinking and disgusting revelry.

Herod's vassals had learned from experience that
these celebrations furnished excellent opportunity for
them to ask for some favor which Herod had refused
them in the past. While he was still sober enough to
understand what was expected of him but drunk enough
to feel that all the world was his to parcel out as he
pleased, he was likely to grant favors which he might
afterward regret but which, once promised in the presence of his guests, he would not recall.

Herodias had looked forward to the event with disgust and some uneasiness. There was no telling what

Herod might do or say when he was half drunk and their plans were at the point where they required discretion. After the return of Nereus, however, she was eager for the celebration. It would fit in perfectly with her scheme concerning Mara and the Baptist.

John the Baptist had been arrested and imprisoned in the fortress of Machaerus. A few days before the feast he was transferred at her insistence to the dungeon beneath the palace at Tiberias. Shortly before Herod's birthday Herodias' young daughter Salome arrived at the palace. Her mother had sent for her.

Salome had the dark beauty of Herodias, who, knowing Herod as she did, realized that her own ripe charms might not survive contrast with the youthful charms of her daughter, so the girl had been living with a relative.

While they sat and talked together Herodias observed with satisfaction Salome's beauty and grace. Salome had been a skillful dancer since her childhood and as they talked and Herodias told her part of the reason she had sent for her, the older woman was glad that under her influence Salome had been taught to dance.

"This birthday is to be a very special occasion," Herodias said, "and I want your dancing to please him more than any other entertainment he has hired. This is to be a surprise, but I want it to be something quite daring. Do something for me and then we can decide just what I want you to do."

Salome began to dance as she hummed a little tune, keeping time to the music, but the performance did not seem to satisfy Herodias.

"This won't do," Herodias remarked. "Herod would

be weary before you were half finished. I want something more daring. Haven't you something else?"

"Yes," Salome said with a shrug, "but I don't think you'll like it. It's a slave dance. I learned it from a Nubian slave, just for fun, but I'd never dare do it in public."

"Let's see it," Herodias insisted.

Slowly the girl began a vulgarly suggestive dance. In spite of herself Herodias felt her cheeks flushing, yet when Salome finished, she said decisively, "That will do perfectly."

"Mother! You don't really mean it?" Salome was horrified.

"I mean exactly that," Herodias declared emphatically. "I want you to please Herod so well that he'll be willing to give you anything you ask for, and by the time I'm ready for you to dance for him only a dance like that could please him."

Salome was serious. "It must be something terribly important. What is it?"

"The head of John the Baptist."

"Who is he?" asked Salome, staring wide-eyed at her mother.

"He's a fool who talked too much," Herodias replied through tight lips.

"If he's talked too much, why doesn't Herod have him beheaded without having to be tricked into doing it?" Salome argued.

"Because Herod's afraid of him. He thinks the man is a prophet. This's the only plan I can think of to get rid of that fellow. That's why you mustn't fail."

Salome listened gravely while Herodias outlined her plan. She was accustomed to crime and intrigue in court circles but this was something so sinister that it shocked and frightened her. Surely her mother must be a little mad or she could never plan a deed like this. An evil demon sent by some angry god must have taken possession of her. The girl did not dare to refuse Herodias' orders for she had no desire to have her mother's anger turned upon her.

"You're not happy, Mother, are you?" she asked during a silence which followed, while she gazed into her mother's gloomy face.

"Is anyone ever really happy?" Herodias sighed.

"You were when you were in love with Father and we were all together. All of us were happy then. None of us has been happy since then. How I wish you'd never left him!"

"I didn't bring you here to discuss that!" Herodias cried harshly.

She sat for a long time after Salome had left her. She was thinking of what the girl had said; thinking of a past she had tried to forget; thinking of a future she was afraid to face. Salome's words brought back memories which she had not allowed herself to dwell upon but which now overwhelmed her. What was wrong with her? She had never been more utterly miserable, more keenly aware of the emptiness of her life. Would a queen's crown fill that emptiness? Would it wipe out memories or bring peace? There was no alternative but to go on.

Herod's feast was to begin at noon and would last into

the small hours of the morning. Rare vines and flowers hung from the palace windows and lined the vast marble banquet hall where long tables stood laden with silver and golden goblets and baskets of fruit and flowers.

The guests arrived early, each hoping for the place of honor nearest Herod. It was also a vantage point for anyone who might have a favor to ask. As the feast began Herodias sat unseen behind the shrubs near a curtained doorway, watching Herod and waiting for the time when he should be in the most receptive mood for her plan. She was never present at these feasts for no respectable woman attended them.

Wine flowed freely; coarse jests were passed about and greeted by loud laughter. Nubian dancers presented fantastic, barbaric dances. A miniature gladiatorial combat was staged and two combatants fought to the death.

When the guests began to tire of the entertainment, when their appetites were satiated with the rich food and when wine began to stir their blood to wilder beating, Herod gave a signal and slave girls from Arabia were brought in.

The babel increased. The air was rent with the screams of girls, hoarse laughter and loud voices, and the faint strains of music which formed a weird background for the chorus.

Nauseating disgust swept over Herodias as she watched the scene and she wavered for a moment in her purpose—but only for a moment. This was the struggle between her own will and that of Herod. This scheme had become an obsession, but she was determined not to abandon the plot.

At last when the noise had subsided somewhat, when the slave girls had been dragged from the scene and the guests had resumed their eating and drinking, Herodias decided that the time had come. Herod had not yet succumbed to the drunken stupor which had already overtaken some of his guests, but he was in a frame of mind wherein he was confident that gifts were his to bestow for the asking. Some scheming guest had just asked for a favor and Herod had granted it. Herodias gave a signal.

Two trumpets sounded. Their loud blare startled the guests who were sober enough to know what was taking place. Herod turned in surprise toward the curtained archway where the trumpeters stood. The curtains parted and four slaves entered bearing a huge shell. They stopped before Herod and one of them proclaimed in loud tones, "The lady Herodias sends a birthday greeting to her lord."

The shell began to open and there was a gasp of surprise as Salome stepped from the shell. Her long black hair was held in place by a fillet of pearls. About her throat was a necklace of pearls with long ropes extending to her wrists. At her waist was a narrow belt of the same pearl beads with ropes which reached to her knees.

Herod gazed fatuously at her while his guests stared open-mouthed as she began the sinuous movements of the dance. It was a novelty to see the daughter of Herodias debase herself for their entertainment.

As Herodias watched her, her face paled and horror swept over her. Why had she done this? She had an impulse to rush in and take the girl from this lewd assembly, but it was too late now. She couldn't retreat. Her fascinated gaze turned from Salome to Herod and his guests. She could read what lay behind those leering eyes and smirking lips. Tensely she watched Herod and a slow smile of satisfaction twisted her lips as she observed his face, his strained interest, for she knew that her plan was succeeding. If the situation should get out of hand, she was prepared to enter the room and take command of it to protect Salome, even though it would mean the end of her scheme concerning the Baptist.

At last the dance was finished and Salome fell with sinuous grace at Herod's feet.

"Have I pleased you, Herod?" she asked in throaty tones.

"Yes!" he cried, and bent over her.

She evaded his arms and sat upon her knees before him. "I'd do anything to please you," she murmured. "Did I really dance well?"

"You pleased me more than any of these hired entertainers." Again he tried to take her in his arms and kiss her.

"If I pleased you better than those entertainers whom you paid, don't you think it would be generous of you to give me some little token of your pleasure instead of demanding more of me?" she asked as her lips puckered into a pout. "You're so wonderful and so generous," she murmured.

"I'll give you anything you want," he said as he beamed upon her with his bloodshot eyes. "A bracelet, a ring, an anklet—or all of them!"

She shook her head. "I have plenty of those."

"Well, what do you want?"

She sighed wistfully. "Something that would prove that you really are pleased with me, but something you might not want to give me."

"Name it and I'll give it to you," he told her, with a sweep of his hand.

"Is that a promise?" She smiled archly, trying to keep her exultation from betraying itself in her voice.

"I swear it!"

"Even if it is very expensive?" she persisted as a wave of relief swept over her. He had already uttered his oath and she knew that her mother's purpose was achieved.

"Even if it is half my kingdom!" He felt as if he were already king of the entire world.

"You're wonderful!" She kissed his hand, then turned to the others. "Isn't he wonderful? He's promised me anything I want."

The guests were watching with interest that varied according to the stages of their sobriety. This would be something to talk about for a long time to come.

Salome turned to Herod and spoke in lower tones. "The greatest thing I could ask for would be your happiness, Herod. That's why I'm going to ask to have one of your most dangerous enemies put out of the way. I want his life."

Herod frowned, sensing some trick, but his befuddled

brain refused to function. "What do you mean?" he asked.

"I want the head of John the Baptist," she said slowly.

He stared at her with bleary eyes. "I see it all now! It was a trick! I might have known when you came here. I won't give it to you!"

He rose and pushed her roughly from him. With a quick, lithe movement she was at his side again.

"Will you be forsworn in the presence of your guests?" she asked. "You swore to give me what I asked for." She lowered her voice. "I'm thinking only of your safety. John the Baptist threatens it. You know that or you would never have arrested him. You now have a good excuse to get rid of him. Blame it on me and it will be easy for you. And some day Tiberius will thank you."

"Get out of here!" he cried in a rage. His face was mottled and splotched, and pallor showed beneath the flush of liquor. "It was all a trick of that mother of yours. Get out!"

As Salome disappeared between the curtains Herod walked unsteadily across the room and out into the corridor. Regret for his foolish oath, rage at the trick that had been played upon him and disappointment at the sudden end to his enjoyment of the feast seethed within him.

Salome met her mother outside the door. "I've made a failure, after all, haven't I?" she whispered.

"No. You succeeded beautifully," Herodias assured her. "He's given his oath. The rest will be easy. Just leave him to me."

She slipped her mantle about Salome's shoulders and the girl disappeared down the corridor. Herodias gave a whispered order to the guard standing at the stairway leading to the dungeon and waited for Herod's approach.

"I thought I'd find you somewhere near!" Herod cried as he saw her.

"I was watching Salome dance," she said quietly.

"Yes, you were watching—to see that your trick worked, you schemer! But your scheming has gone too far!"

"When you're sober you'll realize that this is the best thing that could have happened for us both."

"I'm sober enough now to know why you insisted upon having the Baptist transferred to the dungeon here, so that he'd be near at hand when you put your scheme through. Well, it isn't going to work because I won't kill him!"

"Let's forget about the Baptist, Herod," she said soothingly. "You can decide later whether you want to stand forsworn before all your friends. There's something else down in the dungeon besides the Baptist that you ought to know about. Come down there with me. I want you to find out for yourself what you wouldn't believe if I told you."

"Don't speak in riddles. What is it?"

"It's about Mara," she told him.

"What have you done to her?" he cried, with rising wrath.

"Nothing. It's what she's done for herself that I want you to see and hear. Come with me and be sure not to

make a sound. None of the prisoners must know that
we're there."

"What is this, some new trick?" he asked suspiciously.

"No, Herod. Come with me and you'll hear what I
mean. We may have to wait a while, but you'll know
what you wouldn't believe if I told you. We're going to
be eavesdroppers, so please be quiet. Come on. We must
hurry," she urged gently, tugging at his sleeve.

He hesitated, fearing some new trap, but the mention
of Mara's name filled him with a curiosity he couldn't
resist and he went with her down the dungeon stairway
into the darkness below.

Chapter Fourteen

The Trap

ALL AFTERNOON MARA HAD BEEN WATCHING FROM HER window as the guests arrived for the feast. She could hear the music, the bursts of laughter and occasional loud voices of those already assembled. A horse clattered on the pavement of the courtyard and a white-robed Bedouin, one of the last to arrive, dropped gracefully to the ground and strode in under the huge columns to the banquet hall. He was tall and slim and the way he carried himself reminded her of Judah. She wondered where he was and what he would think when he went back to Jerusalem and found her gone.

Herod's sudden summons had come as a shock, even though she had hoped for it as a means of escape before Judah should return.

Hannah entered, interrupting her reverie, bearing a tray laden with small cakes and fruit and a tempting array of candies.

"Your master sent these to you," Hannah informed her.

Mara could see that Hannah was terribly upset about something. Her hands trembled and there was an air of suppressed terror about her which spoke plainly from her tear-reddened eyes and white face.

"What's the matter, Hannah?" Mara asked anxiously.

"The Baptist has been arrested." Hannah's voice broke in a sob. "He's in the dungeon here beneath the palace."

Sudden fear smote Mara and she stared at Hannah through frightened eyes. "What happened to the Baptist's followers? Did Herod arrest them, too?"

"Only one of them."

"Was—it—Judah?" But even before she saw Hannah's nod she somehow knew that it was. Her thoughts whirled in chaos. That face at the balustrade! It must have been Nereus. And the strange new attitude of friendliness on the part of Herodias since her return. Mara was convinced that Herodias was back of it all.

"How did you find this out?" she asked as she tried to think clearly.

"I heard Mithradas telling one of the other guards about bringing the Baptist here. He said the Baptist and Judah were to stay in the dungeon until they were brought before Herod for trial. He said Judah had been talking too much about putting someone on the throne down in Jerusalem and that he'd be tried for treason."

"That's not the reason they arrested him!" Mara exclaimed. "They did it because Herod knows about us!"

"No, little mistress, no. He doesn't know anything about that. How could he?" Hannah said, trying to calm her fears.

"It must have been Nereus that I saw on the roof that evening."

Hannah sought to reassure her. "It couldn't have been. Herodias would never have risked sending him to spy on you. Besides, if Herod had known, he would have punished you at once."

"Then why have they arrested Judah and let the others go free? Judah hasn't talked any more than the others. That's only an excuse."

"Mithradas said he put up a fight when they took the Baptist. Maybe that's the reason he was the only one arrested."

Mara walked nervously back and forth while Hannah watched her with loving, anxious eyes.

"I've got to do something to help him!" Mara cried frantically.

"What can you do?" Hannah asked helplessly.

"I don't know. But I've got to try to save him. You know very well that Herodias will never let the Baptist get out of there alive. If they kill the Baptist, they'll kill Judah and I couldn't stand that! Oh, what can I do? I must do something! I *must!*"

"But you can't let anyone know that you know him, my child!" Hannah expostulated. "It would mean certain death for you both if Herod suspected the truth."

"Yes, I—suppose—it would," Mara conceded, "but I've got to see him! I've got to find out if he knows why they arrested him. Maybe he can suggest something we could do to help him. I must see him!"

"That's too dangerous to even think of. What if they should find you there in the dungeon talking to him?"

"If they're going to kill him, I don't care if they do find me. It doesn't matter very much now what happens to me. But I've got to see him again—just once!"

"How could you ever get past the guards?"

"I don't know. But you go and find out who's in charge of the dungeon. Perhaps I can think of a way to get down there while Herod's at the feast. Hurry, Hannah! Hurry! Please!"

Hannah left reluctantly and Mara began her ceaseless pacing up and down the room. It seemed hours, though it was only a short time, before Hannah returned.

"Mithradas is on guard this afternoon," Hannah informed her.

"That's fine!" cried Mara in relieved tones. "Mithradas is your friend. He'll help us."

"I don't know whether he's a friend of mine or not," Hannah said as she shook her head slowly. "He's pretended to be my friend but I don't trust him. Sometimes I've had a feeling that he's been trying to use me to find out what's going on in here. He may be a spy for Herodias."

"You've only imagined that. He's done many favors for you. Go and tell him you heard what he said about the Baptist and Judah. Tell him that Judah is a childhood friend of mine. Beg him to let me see him for just a little while. Oh, tell him anything but make him let me go down there! If you think money will help, here's all I have." She gave Hannah a purse full of coins. "Go on! Hurry! And don't come back until you've persuaded him to let me go down there!"

Hannah returned sooner than Mara had hoped.

"What luck did you have?" she asked eagerly.

"Mithradas promised that you could see Judah," Hannah replied gravely.

"When? When? When?" Mara asked, shaking Hannah by her shoulders.

"He said he'd send you word when he thought it would be safe for you to go. The corridor to the dungeon isn't far from the banquet hall and he must be sure there'll be no chance of your being seen. It will be late this evening."

"Thanks, Hannah!" She put her arm affectionately about the woman. "Thanks! It was good of you to do this for me." Tears filled her eyes.

"I wish you wouldn't go, my child," Hannah protested. "I don't like the looks of things."

"What do you mean?"

"Somehow Mithradas seemed too willing to try to arrange the favor I asked. It wasn't so much what he said but the way he acted. He said he felt sorry for the poor boy because he was so young and had no friends here. He was glad to know you were his friend. I can't picture Mithradas feeling that sorry for anyone, least of all a Jew. I had a feeling that he'd been expecting me all the time and that he was just acting."

"I've got to take the chance anyway and I hope you're wrong. But I've got to see Judah."

At last the message from Mithradas came and Mara made her way cautiously down the corridor leading to the dungeon. At the top of the steps she saw Mithradas.

"You can't stay long," he whispered. "I'll give you

warning when to leave. The cell is at the first turn to the right."

"Thank you, Mithradas," Mara murmured. "You've been so good to do this for me. I hope I can do something for you some day."

The corridor was dimly lighted by a torch and as she stopped in front of the cell she could see through the grated door a dim form lying on a crude pallet.

"Judah!" she called softly with her face close to the iron grating.

He got up suddenly, with a gasp of surprise, and came to the door.

"Don't make any noise," she cautioned.

She reached through the door and caught both his hands.

"How on earth did you get here?" he asked as his hands closed over hers.

His question left her cold with fear. She had forgotten she would have to explain her presence here. Of course he thought she was still in Jerusalem! Frantically she groped for some plausible explanation.

"Samuel had to come to Galilee and Rachel and I came with him. When we got here I heard about your arrest and I've been trying to get a chance to see you. Mithradas is a friend of Hannah's and she persuaded him to let me slip in here for a little while."

He seemed to believe the lie and she was thankful.

"Isn't it dangerous for you to be here without Herod's permission?" he asked.

"What do I care for danger so long as I see you?" she murmured. "Why have they arrested you, Judah?"

"I suppose it was because I put up a fight when they
arrested the Baptist. They struck him so viciously I had
to fight them, the brutes! They had no other reason to
arrest me that I know of."

"Oh, I'm so afraid that Herod will do something terrible to you!" Mara cried.

"He has no right to keep us here long, for neither
of us has committed any crime and we ought to have
an early hearing. But you never can tell what he may
do."

"Herodias hates the Baptist and she'll never let him
get out of here alive if she can help it. And if the Baptist
is punished with death, you may be, too, just because
you're one of his disciples."

"We won't have cause to be afraid of either Herod or
Herodias much longer, my darling," he assured her.
"The Messiah will soon be on his throne and Herod
may be a prisoner in his own dungeon before very long."

"But the Messiah may not come to his throne in time
to save you," she cried with a little catch in her voice.

"The Baptist says he may declare himself any day."

"I hope he will do it soon, before they have a chance
to harm you!"

"I was thinking about you when I heard your voice,
and I thought I must be dreaming," he said tenderly.
"Do you remember that dream I had when you first
kissed me?"

"As if I could ever forget it!"

"It was a most unmaidenly kiss." He laughed softly,
then drew her closer to the bars. "I love you so!" he said
gently.

A noise startled them and Mara, suddenly terrified, caught her breath. "What was that?" she cried nervously.

"Only a rat. I have plenty of them to keep me company."

She clung to him desperately between the bars. "O Judah, if anything should happen to you, I wouldn't want to live."

"Nothing will happen to me, darling. Don't be afraid. Something tells me I'll soon be out of here. Then I'll hold you to your promise to have our betrothal ceremony performed."

"Oh, I hope it's true! I hope it's true! I love you so—more than life or death or all that life could hold. I don't want to live without you!"

"Kiss me," he whispered.

Just then Mithradas called to her to come at once and with a whispered word she left him.

A few moments later Herod, followed by Herodias, mounted the stairway leading from the dungeon. Herod's bloodshot eyes blazed with fury and his face was mottled with rage.

"Why didn't you let me go when I wanted to?" he stormed. "I would have choked the life out of her while she was kissing that fellow."

"Would that have been in keeping with your position?" she asked. She could scarcely conceal the smile of satisfaction that flickered across her dark face. Mara had fitted in with her schemes as perfectly as if she had rehearsed the part.

"My position! Bah!" Herod fumed. "She should have

been killed on the spot. She's made a fool of me and she's going to pay for it with her life!"

"I could think of a much better way to punish her than choking her to death," Herodias offered.

"You're always thinking of some plan that's better than mine! I don't want to hear it."

"Let's not talk about it now," she said soothingly. "Go back to your party and enjoy yourself. We can talk about it later. There's plenty of time."

"I'm not going back there," he announced. "You spoiled the whole affair with that bloody scheme of yours about the Baptist."

Herod left her and she sought Mithradas, who was waiting for her.

"That was good work, Mithradas," she commended. "My plan succeeded even better than I'd hoped. I haven't forgotten that promotion I promised you."

"Thanks, my lady," murmured Mithradas, but as she turned away, a look of contempt flashed in Mithradas' eyes.

Chapter Fifteen

The Judgment

HEROD'S JUDGMENT HALL WAS NEVER A PLEASANT PLACE, but on this afternoon it seemed more dismal than usual. The two tall chairs at the end of the room faced a rack and a scourging post. The one single window let in a ghastly light which shone faintly on the gray walls and the dark flagstone floor.

As Herod entered with Herodias, his mood seemed tuned to the scene which confronted him. There was a scowl on his blotched face. His egotism had suffered a rude shock. He had been made a fool of and, worst of all, by a slave upon whom he had lavished every favor. He had loved Mara with a love that was different from anything he had ever known—deeper, more enduring, more satisfying. About her he had built all his dreams and secret hopes. It was not flattering to know that she had turned from him to some unknown with neither rank nor wealth.

He had been ashamed not to keep the oath he had made to Salome and had ordered the Baptist beheaded. Fear of the consequences of this deed and the knowledge of Mara's unfaithfulness made him peevish and sullen.

Herodias silently took her seat beside him. She was clad in a long robe of violet silk and her hair was bound by a triple band of amethysts that fitted like a cap across her forehead and head. Her lips were bright with carmine and her dark skin glowed with a touch of rouge. Her eyes were gleaming with triumph. This was to be the closing act of the drama which she and Nereus had planned. Mara would soon be disposed of. Some childish desire to appear beautiful in Herod's eyes today had prompted Herodias to dress as she had, and she felt piqued and disappointed because he had not even favored her with a glance.

"I don't see any reason for you to be so glum," she remarked after she had seated herself.

"You wouldn't!" He turned on her furiously. "You tricked me into doing something I didn't want to do, just to have your own way. How do I know that this business here this afternoon isn't another of your schemes, just a trick to get rid of Mara?"

"I'm not clever enough to make your slave pretend to fall in love with someone else." She laughed. "You flatter me."

A spasm of rage distorted his face. "No, you couldn't do that," he conceded. "She's brought this on herself and she's going to pay for it!"

He gave an order to a slave standing near by. The slave went out and returned with Judah. Judah's hands were bound behind him but he walked with firm, assured tread. The slave pushed him down on a bench near Herod. Herod's angry gaze traveled slowly over Judah, noting his dark attractive face and the strong muscular figure, and his wrath rose higher.

"You dog of a Jew!" he cried. "You're going to pay for what you've done!"

Judah returned his gaze with steady eyes. "If I've broken the law I have a right to be tried according to the law, Tetrarch," he said quietly.

"Before I finish with you, you'll be screaming for mercy instead of demanding your rights!"

He gave a curt order and the slave again left the room.

Mara was in her room trying to work on a bit of tapestry but her hands fell idle in her lap. Though she tried to comfort herself with the hope Judah had given her, some vague premonition of evil made her restless and afraid. Presently there was a knock on the door, interrupting her unhappy thoughts.

When Mara answered the knock and she saw the slave standing there in the doorway, something told her even before he delivered his message that tragedy was in store for her. She tried to still the beating of her heart as she followed the slave to the judgment hall. When the door opened into the gloomy room she stood for a moment while her eyes became accustomed to the dim light.

Herod turned and looked at her and in spite of himself his heart beat faster and a light leaped into his eyes. How lovely she was! She was clad in soft gray with a band of dull green about her waist and her reddish-gold hair fell in two loose coils across her shoulders.

She saw Judah and she knew that at last he would know the truth about her. Her heart seemed to stop beating and her breath came in suffocating gasps. When her eyes fell upon Herodias' face, with its look of satisfied triumph, the girl realized that she was in a trap. She advanced slowly to Herod and as she passed Judah he saw her and gave a gasp of surprise.

"Mara!" he ejaculated in horrified amazement.

With the desperation of despair she sought to save him from whatever might involve her and she ignored his startled cry. She wouldn't trust herself to look at him. She stopped before Herod and waited with dull despair for what might follow.

"Speak, girl!" cried Herod. "Don't stand there gaping like a fool!"

"What do you want me to say, master?" she asked in low tones. "You sent for me."

Judah stared at her in bewildered astonishment. She had called Herod "Master!" His thoughts whirled in dazed confusion as Herod spoke and he listened with growing horror to what followed.

"Yes, I sent for you so that you could feast your eyes on this lover of yours. When I've finished with him, he won't be fit for you or anyone else to look at."

Mara turned slowly and looked at Judah. His eyes, revealing his doubt of her and fear for her and a desperate effort to understand, held hers in spite of her unwillingness to face them. She longed to throw herself into his arms, to beg him for a chance to explain, to plead for the love which she knew would soon give way to loathing, but, like an automaton, she turned from him to Herod again.

"There must be some mistake," she said slowly and painfully. "He's no lover of mine, master. I never saw him before."

"Don't lie to me, girl," Herod rasped, "or I'll have your tongue torn out. I heard you two in the dungeon last night, so don't try to pretend you don't know him. I was down there listening and I heard every word you two said!"

Mara caught her breath with a gasp. Hannah had been right about Mithradas! He had led her into this trap and Judah had been caught in it also. A death too horrible to contemplate would be the end for both of them. Desperately she tried to save him. Controlling her fear and trying to speak quietly, she stared at Herod with wide eyes.

"I wasn't in the dungeon last night, master. I didn't even know this man was there. It's a trick someone is trying to play to make you angry with me."

Her appealing beauty, the love he still had for her and his suspicion of Herodias made him almost believe her. He turned angrily to Herodias.

"Is she telling the truth?" he demanded. "Was this a trick of yours?"

"Yes, it was, master," Mara interrupted frantically. "She's only trying to poison your mind against me. She hates me because you've been good to me. I wasn't in the dungeon. I swear it! I never saw this man before!"

Herodias laughed mirthlessly. "Take a look at that fellow," she advised Herod coldly. "His face will tell you whether it was a trick of mine or not."

Herod turned and looked at Judah. The shock and horror of what he had heard and the truth which was being revealed to him combined to betray him, even though, at Herodias' words, he tried to recover himself.

"Speak, fellow!" Herod cried. "You'll admit the truth if you want to save yourself from torture. What have you to say?"

Judah glanced swiftly at Mara but she evaded his eyes. "Nothing," he answered.

"I'll make you speak, you stubborn fool!" He had seen the glance and it roused him to added fury. "Your tongue was loose enough last night when you were babbling to this slave of mine. Didn't you know that she was my concubine and that it meant death to you to dare to make love to her?"

"It isn't true!" Judah cried through pale lips. "It can't be true! She isn't your concubine, you——"

"Master, don't believe what anyone has told you!" Mara interrupted wildly. "I don't love this man. I swear I don't love anyone but you!"

She dropped to her knees at Herod's feet and caressed his hand that lay upon the arm of the chair.

"Don't believe what they say! You know it isn't true." Her voice was low and throbbing and her gaze lured him as it always had. He extended his hand impulsively toward her head but Herodias' voice cut like a blade across the sudden impulse of tenderness.

"There are ways of making her confess the truth if you feel that I haven't told it. Unless you prefer the testimony of Mithradas."

He rose and pushed Mara roughly from him.

"She shall confess! I'll make her confess! The scourge will force the truth from her."

He gave an order and a slave advanced toward Mara.

Judah burst out frantically, "Don't do that to her, you brute! If you must torture someone, torture me!"

"So! We're beginning to find out the truth." A distorted smile twisted Herod's lips. "This promises to be interesting."

Mara turned to Judah and asked in broken tones, "Why did you say that? I was trying to save you."

He stared at her silently, a stricken look in his dark eyes.

Herod's brutal laughter burst forth.

"Been trying to save him, have you? He asked to take your place, so I'll let him do it. Take him over there and put him on the rack. Let him know how it feels to have his joints stretched," he commanded.

Two attendants came forward and took Judah to the rack and Mara threw herself at Herod's feet.

"O master, don't do that! Don't do that!" she cried in an agony of entreaty. "I'll confess anything. Torture me or kill me, but don't torture him! It was all my fault. I lied to him. He didn't know I was your concubine. He didn't know I belonged to you!"

Herod regarded her silently. Then his eyes traveled to Judah, who had been strapped to the rack. He gave a signal and the screws were slowly turned. Each turn of the screws stretched the joints of arms and hands and legs until the tendons were almost torn loose. Great drops of sweat stood on Judah's face and he groaned faintly through clenched teeth.

At the sound of his groans Mara turned and looked at him, then groveled at Herod's feet, crying hysterically and begging for mercy.

"Are you willing to take his place?" Herod's merciless voice taunted her.

She took another horrified look at Judah as the screws were given another turn and his twisted lips uttered another moan of pain. Then she covered her face with her hands.

"Yes! Yes! I'll take his place," she sobbed. "Stop torturing him, please! Please!" She raised a tear-drenched face to Herod.

Herod laughed. "He doesn't seem to be enjoying the situation."

As Judah's faint groans came to her again, Mara turned terror-stricken eyes to him, then crumpled in an unconscious heap.

"Stop!" Herod cried. "She's fainted. Release him and bring him here."

Judah was released but his tortured muscles refused to support him and he fell to the floor. The slaves half carried, half dragged him to the bench and dropped him upon it where he lay scarcely conscious. One of the attendants brought in a pungent drug and held it under Mara's nose. After a few breaths she showed signs of returning consciousness.

"Get up and take a look at your lover now," Herod commanded. "Isn't he a sight to thrill any woman's heart? Go and tell him good-bye before I finish with you. I'll be good enough to let you do that."

Mara rose slowly and went to Judah. Her face was ashen while tears ran unheeded down her face.

"Judah!" she called in a low voice.

He opened his eyes and looked at her and she shrank from what she saw in his gaze.

"Don't look at me like that!" she begged. "Please don't! I don't blame you for hating me but I never dreamed it would end like this. I would have killed myself before I'd have let this happen to you. I deceived you because I loved you so and I knew you'd despise me if you knew the truth. I—I—was hoping for some miracle to happen so that you'd never know. Oh, I love you so! I'll love you with every beat of my heart until—until—the—end."

He stared at her through eyes dimmed with suffering, then burst out bitterly, "And I was fool enough to call you a pure lily!"

She recoiled as if he had struck her. "Is that all you have to say to me, Judah?" she murmured.

He closed his eyes as a spasm of pain crossed his face.

"He'll have plenty to say presently," Herod cried.

"Take her over there," he ordered a slave, "and tie her to the whipping post."

The slave stripped Mara of her outer garments and tied her by her hands to the post. At the first blow of the lash the cruel bits of steel cut into her flesh. Blood trickled in a tiny stream down her back. Judah jumped from the bench with a sudden spurt of strength and darted past the guard toward Herod. He had almost reached the startled Herod before he was jerked back roughly. He fought with the frenzy of a wild beast until his weakened strength was spent and he stood panting and breathless.

"Let her go! Let her go!" he cried.

"Lay it on harder, you fool!" Herod called to the slave.

The lash cut the air with a faint swish and struck

Mara's back with a thud. Her faint scream died in a gurgling gasp as she fainted again. Her body sagged limply against the bloodstained post, held there by her hands strapped to the leather thongs. At an order from Herod she was released and laid at his feet. Restoratives were administered while he waited impatiently. He turned to Judah with a mocking laugh.

"You should feel happy now. You've had your revenge. She has you to thank for this."

Judah stared dully at Mara. Physical and mental torture had robbed him of the power to think clearly. His mind was beclouded. He had a feeling that he had suddenly become unbalanced, that he was losing his mind, that all this was not real but a nightmare to torture his mind as his body had been tortured.

"I haven't finished with you yet," Herod's mocking voice continued. "When you see what I've done to your master, you can remember that you and this girl are responsible for what's happened to him."

Somewhere in Judah's dim consciousness Herod's foreboding threat brought an added twinge of suffering, but he couldn't think clearly or understand why he should feel this way.

Mara at last opened her eyes and looked dazedly about her while a low moan of pain escaped her lips. Herod gave a signal and one of the guards left the room. He returned in a moment bearing a huge platter containing something covered with a white cloth.

As he crossed to Judah and removed the cloth, Herod cried, "A betrothal present to you from the Governor of Galilee. Take a look and remember that it was you and

Mara who made this gift possible. If you hadn't fallen in love with my concubine, this would never have happened."

Judah raised his eyes and stared into the sightless eyes of John the Baptist. For a moment he gazed with wide eyes and parted lips at the gruesome object. Then a terrible cry tore itself from his throat.

"It's my master! It's my master!" he shrieked wildly.

"I thought his features would be familiar to you," Herod taunted. "Remember that he has you to thank for his death."

Judah turned once more to the lifeless head and he cried hoarsely, "No, no! I didn't kill him! I didn't do it! It was you, you murderer! You've murdered him! You've killed my master!"

Something seemed to have snapped within his brain as he uttered those words. His voice was hard and high-pitched and a wild light came into his eyes. He was possessed of sudden strength and sprang toward Herod's throat with a shrill savage scream. He seemed changed in a moment from a bewildered man to a maddened beast intent upon killing. He seized Herod in his grasp and dragged him from the chair. The guards rushed up but he fought them madly, viciously, with a strength that baffled and terrified them. They drove him back from the frightened Herod with the points of their spears. The combined efforts of them all could scarcely hold him. He raged and screamed and fought as Herod looked on, completely upset by this sudden turn of events.

"He's lost his reason!" Herodias exclaimed uneasily.

"Yes. He's gone mad." Herod's face was white. Fear filled his soul at the sight of Judah's wild eyes, his bestial cries and superhuman strength. "Take him away and chain him in the dungeon," he ordered shakily, as he heard his bestial cries.

"Aren't you going to finish this affair?" Herodias asked in anxious tones.

"No," he snapped. "He's lost his mind. Do you expect me to execute a madman and bring down the curse of the gods upon me?"

"Mara's not mad. What are you going to do with her?" Herodias persisted. There was a sullen brooding light in her eyes as she watched the soldiers struggling to get Judah through the narrow door. This sudden upset to her plans displeased her greatly.

"I don't know," Herod answered morosely. "I'll decide that tomorrow. It looks as if the gods have turned against me."

"Nonsense! You should get this thing over with, since you've started it," she urged.

He rose without answering as the soldiers succeeded in getting Judah out of the door. When he had heard the huge door of a near-by cell clank shut and the lock turn, he left the room. As Herodias followed, there was a frown upon her face and her lips were pressed into a thin straight line.

The door closed upon them, leaving Mara alone with only the guards standing outside the door. Her low sobs broke the sudden silence.

Chapter Sixteen

The Sentence

THE MORNING WAS CHILL AND GLOOMY FOR A SUMMER day. Low-lying clouds, driven by an easterly wind, scudded across a dark sky.

As Herod entered the room he drew his mantle about him and shivered. His face bore the marks of heavy drinking and a sleepless night. An evil light glimmered in his eyes and the cruel lines about his mouth were accentuated by his tight-drawn lips. He dispatched a servant with the order to bring Mara and he waited impatiently for her coming.

After he had left the torture chamber he had tried to drink himself into forgetfulness, but drinking had served only to further irritate his overwrought nerves and he had paced the floor for hours, unable to sleep. His superstitious fears terrified him. The gods would punish anyone who harmed a madman and he felt as if all the gods on Olympus had turned from him in anger.

The memory of the head of John the Baptist lying on the silver charger haunted him. He could not forget those eyes. To his liquor-sodden brain it seemed that there was an accusing, warning light in their sightless depths.

To add to his uneasiness, the night was made hideous by Judah's shrill, unearthly cries. Judah's cries brought thoughts of Mara and thoughts of her brought a sense of loss which added to his unhappiness. He had not realized how much he had loved her until now when she was lost to him. A savage desire possessed him to make her suffer torture worse than she had already endured.

Presently the door opened and Mara entered. She was clad in a dark brown robe. She was weak and exhausted from suffering. There were deep circles beneath her eyes and her full red lips drooped. Her very helplessness seemed to call forth in Herod some new protectiveness. She walked with slow, faltering step and stood before him with hands loosely clasped before her, without raising her eyes from the floor.

"What a fool you were to have thrown away my love!" he cried impulsively. He longed to take her in his arms and feel once more the warmth of her lips and to assure her that he would never hurt her again.

She raised her eyes and stared dully at him.

"I was a fool not to have killed myself before I ever consented to be your slave," she said slowly.

The door had opened and Herodias had entered unobserved. Her face was pale and she also bore the effects of a sleepless night. As she heard Herod's words she realized that he still loved Mara and a new wave of hatred for the girl swept over her. A faint fear seized her. Vacillating as Herod was, even yet he might give Mara another chance. If the girl had any wits at all she'd make the most of this opportunity and if she did, then all of Herodias' carefully-made plans would fail. When she heard Mara's answer, however, a smile flitted across her face. Mara had lost her one chance.

"Your slave isn't very grateful for all your past favors," Herodias remarked as she approached Herod.

Herod turned to her with an impatient frown as she sat down beside him.

"She's more faithful to the new love than she was to the old, even though it brought her a beating," she continued.

Herod laughed harshly. "She must have enjoyed his serenade last night." He turned to Mara. "Did you hear him?" he asked.

"Yes," she said, through bloodless lips.

"Those were the cries of a madman, Mara. Your lover is no longer human. He's become a wild beast."

She raised her stricken eyes to his face but said nothing.

"He's saved his life by going mad," Herod continued. "I can't execute him now as I had planned to do."

"It would be merciful to kill him," she said dully.

"I have no desire to be merciful. What I want is to make you suffer for your unfaithfulness to me. And he's going to help me do that. It'll be much more satisfactory than killing you both as I had intended to do."

She stared at him without answering.

"Your lover is already on his way to Decapolis. He shall live there like the wild beast that he has become until the gods have mercy on him and take his life. He shall depend upon you for his food. As for his clothing, I don't think he'll need any. He's already torn off every rag. You're going to earn your living—and his, too."

He saw the new fear that leaped into her eyes and it pleased him. "From now on you shall be known from one end of Palestine to the other as Mara the Wanderer. You threw away my love for this fellow. Now go and sell your kisses and yourself on the highways for the money to buy his food."

"I won't do it! You can't make me!" she cried.

"You'll learn that I can. One of my soldiers shall follow you constantly to see that you obey my orders. You won't be allowed to remain more than three days in any one place. You shall travel until the very thought of the road sickens you. Once a month you shall take food to your lover. He'll be a pleasant sight, I'm sure, and I know you'll enjoy those visits. I want you to remember, every day and hour, what you might have been if you had been faithful to me."

"You may as well kill me now," she said wearily. "I'll never, never do it."

"No, I won't kill you. That would be too merciful. Death will be only too welcome for you from now on. That's what I want. I want you to pray for death and long for it and still be afraid to die. If you don't obey the sentence, then that lover of yours shall suffer torture such as you've never seen. I won't kill him, but I'll make him wish he were dead. Every day you refuse to carry out my bidding, he shall be stretched on the rack until he's a helpless mass of broken joints. And you shall be scourged to the limit, every day you disobey me. Now get out unless you'd rather begin the torture now! Your guard is waiting outside for you. You're going to begin your wanderings today."

Mara looked at him silently for a moment, then walked slowly from the room. Herod sat watching her and even then the desire possessed him to call her back. As the door closed behind her, Herodias' bitter laughter echoed through the room.

Chapter Seventeen

The Long Road

MARA WENT OUT, DAZED AND BEWILDERED, INTO THE cold gray morning. She wandered aimlessly about until, spent and exhausted, she stood beside the lake. The water looked cool and inviting. It would be so easy to slip beneath it and seek forgetfulness. But she couldn't. How cunning Herod had been! He had counted upon her love for Judah, her fear of what would become of him if she killed herself and left him to his fate. How well he had guessed what torture love would be, keeping her alive when she longed desperately to die.

Hour after hour she sat huddled on the shore, lost in the depths of utter despair. The longing to see Judah assailed her. She must see him and be sure that Herod had told her the truth about him. Perhaps it was only a trick to make her suffer more. She must be sure. She went to the bazaar near the market place and sold one of her rings, from among the trinkets Herod had given her, for money to pay her fare across the lake.

Before she reached the top of the rocky slope across the lake, she heard the shrill, eerie cries which seemed to freeze her blood and crush out the last spark of hope.

Then she saw Judah. He was a horrible sight. His body was slashed and cut, and the dried blood, mingled with dirt and small bits of grass, clung to him in a clotted mass. His unshaven face was streaked with dirt and blood. He wandered up and down among the boulders, uttering savage, unearthly cries, heedless that he bruised his body or tore his flesh on the sharp rocks.

A spasm of agony gripped her heart—an agony too deep for tears. As she watched him, it seemed that every emotion was drained from her except bitterness and hate toward the man who was responsible for Judah's condition.

Presently he dropped to the ground as if he had fainted. She started toward him. A soldier appeared and stopped her.

"You can't go any nearer. He'll kill you."

"Then have mercy and let me go to him!" she cried brokenly.

"It's against Herod's orders," the soldier stated.

"Have pity on him and drive your spear through him as he lies there," she begged. "Please! Be merciful and put him out of his misery!"

"And be put to death myself for my trouble?" He laughed harshly. "You talk like a fool. It's Herod's orders for no one to stop here, so get along."

"I couldn't expect pity from anyone who served Herod," she remarked bitterly.

"Rulers aren't supposed to have pity," the soldier informed her.

She looked across the hills and saw the flash of spear

and shield as the sunlight shone upon the sentries stationed there.

"Herod spares no expense or trouble to satisfy his vengeance," she remarked.

"What's the good of his being the Tetrarch if he can't punish those who've offended him?"

She turned and made her way back to the shore. As she returned across the Sea of Galilee and set out toward Jerusalem, a dull apathy settled like a weight upon her. One of Herod's men followed her, never letting her get out of his sight. When she reached Jerusalem, forgetful of the shadowing guard, she went to Rachel's home, hoping against hope that she would find a refuge there, since she was out of Herod's jurisdiction. For a few days peace was allowed her; then her fears and misgivings were realized. One morning a soldier brought Rachel a parchment. She read it aloud to Mara.

"'Pontius Pilate, Governor of Judea, has been informed that in this house, Mara the Wanderer, courtesan, under sentence of Herod, Tetrarch of Galilee, is hiding. If she is allowed to remain, Samuel, the merchant, and Rachel, his wife, shall be considered offenders against the Roman government. As such, both shall be imprisoned and their property shall be confiscated by the Governor of Judea, in the name of Tiberius, Emperor of Rome. Signed Pontius Pilate, Governor of Judea.'"

"What are you going to do, Mara?" asked Rachel, aghast.

"I'll have to go. I can't stay here and bring harm to you," Mara replied.

"Where will you go?" Rachel inquired anxiously.

"Why worry about that?" cried Mara bitterly. "Herod's called me Mara the Wanderer, courtesan. I may as well live up to the name."

"O Mara! Surely you won't do that!"

"What else can I do? I can't kill myself. How I wish I could! But there's Judah, and look what I've brought upon him! There's no other way. I must take to the road. Nothing matters now, anyway."

She removed the veil from her hair and plaited it in two long braids. This braided hair would be the symbol of her calling. Everyone who saw her would know that she was ready to satisfy the desires of any man who wanted her.

"Mara of the megaddela." She laughed harshly, indicating her braided hair. Her face was pale and drawn, while in her eyes there was a reckless light.

"Oh, it's too horrible!" Rachel cried brokenly.

Mara kissed her and held her close for a moment. "Good-bye," she said solemnly. "I—I—don't know when I'll ever see you again, my dear."

She walked slowly down the steps, the sound of Rachel's sobs echoing in her ears, and out upon the white-paved, narrow street. Her lip quivered tremulously and she felt the sting of tears in her eyes as she saw the glances of the men who passed her.

She turned an indifferent eye upon them all as she went aimlessly on her way, but as she walked, horror and revulsion overwhelmed her like a foul flood. She couldn't go through with it! She wouldn't! Judah would have to suffer torture! This was indeed worse than death. She wandered out the Damascus Gate and on the highway. Dusk was falling but she had forgotten time or fatigue, hunger or thirst. Demons seemed to be driving her on her aimless way.

Presently she was made aware of the presence of her guard. He overtook her and stopped her.

"You're not obeying Herod's orders," he reminded her tersely.

She turned upon him with blazing eyes. "I don't intend to obey him! He can kill me, but he can't make me obey him."

"He doesn't want to kill you. But I've had orders to have you scourged if you didn't obey and I've already waited longer than I should have."

"Go ahead and have me scourged. What difference does it make?"

"Have you forgotten the rest of the decree? I'll have to send word tomorrow to the soldiers at Decapolis to capture the madman and put him to torture."

She stared in stricken silence into his hard, uncompromising face. He laughed at the look of utter hopelessness which came into her eyes. "You're in a trap and you'd better make the best of it," he advised.

Sobs tore through her pale lips. "A trap! Yes, I'm in a trap! It's funny, isn't it?" The sobs were drowned in wild, hysterical laughter. "Funny to you and to that fiend in Galilee. But what about me? I should laugh, too, shouldn't I?" Her laughter continued, one wild peal after another, until suddenly she stopped and struck him across the face with all her strength.

He caught her and shook her roughly. "You're not

making it any easier for yourself by acting like this. I should have you flogged for this! I've half a mind to do it myself."

"Easy! Easy!" she mocked. "Do you think anything could ever be easy for me again? Go ahead and flog me. What do I care?"

Someone came toward them on horseback and the guard had no desire to have to make explanations. "Be quiet, you fool, or you'll get worse than a flogging," he warned. "A girl as beautiful as you are ought to have a pretty easy time of it. Rich men will pay you gold. And it will take gold to buy food for that fellow over in Decapolis."

She pushed him from her so violently and unexpectedly that he lost his balance and fell sprawling. As he struggled to his feet, dust-covered and furious, she turned back toward the city, moaning and talking to herself.

"Gold! Gold! I must have gold! But all the gold in the world can't ease this torture in my heart and bring peace to my soul! All the gold in the world can't bring Judah back to me again!"

The guard followed at a safe distance, afraid of another outburst. He had orders, under pain of death, to see that no harm came to her, and he was at a loss to handle this unexpected situation.

A year passed and summer was at hand again. Along the wayside the almond trees were in bloom, showering the ground with a carpet of petals. Flocks of sheep dotted the hillside with flecks of white in the green pasture grounds. On the road to Jerusalem a caravan of heavily-laden camels was raising the dust in a gray cloud.

It was a quiet, peaceful day with scarcely a breeze stirring the olive trees on the rugged slopes beyond the city. But there was no peace in the heart of Mara as she approached Jerusalem. A wild recklessness successfully hid from the casual eye of those who came in contact with her the hopeless misery of her life, the dull ache in her heart and the bitterness of despair that filled her soul.

It seemed, as the months passed, that she had lost her reason. Some said she was possessed of devils; others, that she herself was a devil. None but Mara knew the depths of her own agony.

During the year she had become a familiar figure in eastern Judea and Galilee. Herod's decree had been fulfilled to the last letter. She was still beautiful. Sorrow and suffering had not changed the beauty of feature and form, the wonder of her red-gold hair and her deep-fringed eyes, but in her lovely face appeared lines of hardness and in her eyes shone the spark of a soul aflame with hatred and despair. She was like the beautiful, hardened shell of the girl she had once been.

Each month she had gone to Judah, taking provisions that should have lasted through the month. Every day a guard carelessly tossed him enough food for the day. He would fall upon it, eat until his hunger was satisfied, then scatter the rest over the rocky ground. When he became hungry again he would go about among the rocks, picking up small bits of food wherever he found them.

She determined each time she went that she'd never go back again, that she'd let him starve to death as a merciful way out, yet the thought of Herod's threat and some inner force stronger than her will drove her back.

Judah had become loathsome beyond belief. His long matted hair and beard, vermin-infested and encrusted with dirt, his nails grown like claws, and his body, tanned, scarred and filthy, made him something that would have repulsed the strongest. To her it was worse than torture to look at him. Determined to kill herself afterward, she had tried more than once to kill him, but every effort had failed.

As she made her way along the highway to Jerusalem, her thoughts traveled over the past months. It was not often that she let her thoughts dwell on the past. Seeking forgetfulness, she tried desperately to keep from thinking of herself at all, but when the time approached for her to make her pilgrimage to Judah, and for days afterward, she was tortured by memories that, once awakened, were hard to banish.

This afternoon she traveled the same road over which she had first come to the city. In reality it was but little more than a year, yet to her it seemed ages past. It was on just such a day that she had first seen Judah. She stopped a moment and her gaze traveled over the scene. In spite of herself, tears that she had thought dried forever came to her eyes. It was here that she had stood on that day, admiring the beauty of the panorama before her, the city walls, the towering hills, the white temple in the sunlight.

She saw again in the distance a shepherd leading his

flock toward the fold. She turned wearily away and continued on her way. How foolish to remember when memory brought only agony! She saw a group of men coming up the slope ahead of her and her heart throbbed painfully as she watched them. They were so like that group she had seen on that other day that they might have been ghosts of the past returned to torment her. Her gaze rested upon the leader of the group. There was a majesty and a power about him which she felt unaccountably. She felt as if she had met him before. As he came toward her he raised his eyes and looked at her and then she remembered. He was the same one whom the Baptist had baptized that day on the Jordan and who had stirred her so by his glance that seemed to read her very soul. She could never forget that look!

This time as he looked at her he seemed to see again into her soul and to read there all the degradation of her life. But this time she did not shrink and cower in shame from his all-seeing eyes. She met his gaze with a bold, defiant stare. In her heart there surged a bitter hate for him. This was the man Judah had believed to be the expected Messiah. This was the man who had raised false hopes within her own heart that she might be free!

As they passed her and went down the road, a bitter laugh escaped her lips. What a Messiah he had proved to be! A lowly wanderer preaching by the wayside as John the Baptist had done. What a noble following he had! Humble, poorly-clad men with the stamp of toil upon them!

She continued on her way and the laughter died from her lips as the memory of his face returned to her and the gaze he had bent upon her, that gaze which seemed to penetrate to her very soul.

"He knows what I am," she whispered through pale lips. "But what do I care if he does know? Everyone else in Judea knows that even God Himself has cast me off! What do I care what anyone thinks of me?"

Chapter Eighteen

Another Web Is Woven

HEROD HAD RECEIVED FAITHFUL REPORTS OF MARA'S life. He experienced a certain amount of satisfaction in the knowledge of her suffering, yet deep in his heart there was still a yearning for her, an emptiness without her, which made him miserable and restless.

His political affairs did not serve to make him any happier. His plans for gaining his kingdom had met with a sudden halt in the death of Hasta, his most influential friend at the court of Tiberius, and all his energies and resources had to be rallied to renew the efforts he had thought were ready to be crowned with success.

Many times during the year there had come to him disquieting thoughts of the Baptist. When he least expected it, there came to him the disturbing memory of the Baptist's head upon the platter.

When the fame of Jesus of Nazareth reached him, it brought more disturbing thoughts and more terrible dreams. Herodias spoke to him one day about this new preacher. In her heart there were no disturbing memories, only an increasing annoyance over the growing popularity of this new leader.

"We must do something about this fellow," she said one day, to Herod. "His fame seems to grow by leaps and bounds. If you're not careful, he'll be starting trouble here in Galilee."

"What do you expect me to do about it?" he asked irritably.

"Do something to stop him before his power with the people grows too strong. If you had taken my advice and pushed your cause with Tiberius before Hasta died, you would have been in possession of your kingdom before now. These stupid Jews are beginning to say that this man is the Messiah, just as they did about the Baptist. In their eyes, everyone who comes along with a new message is the Messiah."

A shadow crossed Herod's face. "I'm afraid of him," he muttered. "They say he has a strange power. I wonder if he could be John the Baptist returned from the dead."

"What's the matter with you?" she asked in provoked surprise. "Where did you ever get such nonsense?"

"I don't know. Sometimes I feel as if I were losing my mind."

"You must be, talking about people returning from the dead. What ever put that absurd idea in your head?"

"I—I—dream about him all the time. Sometimes I dream about his returning from the dead to torment me for beheading him."

She observed how Herod had aged, how his continual drinking had left its mark on his once handsome face. A faint contempt tinged her tones as she replied.

"Don't be so foolish! This man is only another fanatic

who would hoodwink these credulous Jews into winning
him a throne."

"They say he's performed marvelous cures."

"Trickery!" she answered scornfully. "Are you going
to sit idly by and let a dog of a Jew steal your throne?"

"I'm not going to let you force me into another murder!" he thundered.

"You're a fool, Antipas," she remarked witheringly.

At the first opportunity she sent for Mithradas.
Though he did not possess the scheming brain that
Nereus had, he had always served her faithfully. She
didn't realize that since that night when Mithradas had
led Mara into the trap in the dungeon his loyalty had
wavered. Since then there had grown within him a
greater feeling of distrust for her than he had ever experienced and coupled with it a greater fear of her than
he had known for anyone. Only by serving her, however, could he hope to obtain the advancement for
which he longed.

She outlined her plan to him. He was to follow the
Nazarene and report his movements to her.

Mithradas demurred. "I'm a soldier, my lady, not a
spy. Can't someone else do this better than I?"

She regarded him with amazed displeasure. It was the
first time he had ever balked at her commands.

"If I had thought there was such a person, I wouldn't
have sent for you," she informed him acidly. "All you
have to do is to keep me informed as to where he is and
what he's doing. That ought to be easy, for his work isn't
done in secret. He preaches where anyone can hear
what he has to say. I want to know the effect of his

preaching upon the people. As for your being a soldier, you're dismissed temporarily from your company. From now on you're to wear civilian clothes. And remember, soldiers who show their unwillingness to obey commands can never expect advancement."

He understood. She had hinted often that there would be another promotion for him if he showed implicit obedience to her orders.

"I'll do my best, my lady," he replied without enthusiasm.

When Mithradas had left she sent for Nereus. During the past few months, when Herod's outbursts of temper became almost unbearable, she had felt a compelling desire for the contact with Nereus. The constancy of his love was soothing to her and a stimulant to her vanity. But she sternly refused to yield to her desire. She determined that she would not be drawn from her purpose by any secret call of her heart. When he appeared, however, she felt her purpose weaken.

"I have another task for you, Nereus," she informed him.

Nereus' voice was gently reproachful. "I'm glad that something calls me to your side, even if it is only a chance to serve you. It's been a long time since you've let me see you."

"I've been busy and I've been worried about so many things," she answered wearily. "You know that."

"Too busy to give an humble palace guard a thought, even though a moment with you meant happiness for days afterward."

"Too busy to think of anything but the constant dan-

gers which seem to rise to threaten me. I thought when
I disposed of the Baptist that we were rid of the last
obstacle to the throne. But these Jews are like weeds. As
fast as one is cut down, another springs up. Have you
heard of Jesus, the Nazarene?"

"Yes. Stories of his cures have spread all over Galilee."

"Stories that must be stopped before it is too late!"

"You can hardly stop him in the way the Baptist was
stopped," he remarked tactlessly.

"A few more remarks like that and I'll think you're as
big a fool as Herod," she blazed, and the angry flash in
her eyes told him that he had made a foolish slip.

"I'm sorry. Forgive me," he said contritely.

"This fellow may not be disposed of in the same way
the Baptist was, but he can be gotten rid of," she informed him. "That's why I've sent for you. I want you to
go down to Jerusalem again for me, Nereus. You will go,
won't you?"

"What am I supposed to do this time?" he asked, with
a frown.

"Just use your wits. I've heard that the Pharisees are
becoming uneasy about the Nazarene. They've held the
whiphand over their people for so long that they'll op-
pose anyone who threatens to deprive them of their
power."

"Yes," he agreed. "They even have Pilate playing into
their hands at times."

"Pilate's a coward and a fool. I want you to go to
Jerusalem and do whatever you can to stir up these self-
righteous fools against the Nazarene; then report back
to me. I want them to condemn him to death. If he's
killed in Jerusalem, Herod will be rid of him without

danger to himself. Since he beheaded the Baptist, he's afraid of his own shadow."

"I've noticed the change in him," Nereus remarked.

"After what happened to the Baptist, it would never do for this new leader to be put to death in Galilee."

"So I'm to be the instrument to bring about his death."

"Are you getting tired of serving me, Nereus?" There was just the right shade of wistfulness in her voice, just the right glow in her eyes.

"No, my queen," he murmured, as he bent toward her. "I shall never tire of serving you. I wouldn't hesitate to kill anyone who stands in the way of your happiness."

"You're wonderful, Nereus," she sighed. "I couldn't live without you."

For the first time in months she allowed him to take her in his arms. As his lips pressed hers, the cold voice of ambition warned her that she was playing with fire which might destroy her, but for the time being she was deaf to the voice of ambition.

After Nereus had gone and she could think clearly, she realized what a foolish thing she had done. Restless discontent took possession of her. The desire for Nereus overwhelmed her while her growing aversion to Herod filled her with a sense of futility. The prospect of being his queen had lost completely the promise it had held for her. If only she could go back to the time before Nereus had come into her life, before Herod had made complete wreck of it! If only she had never known either Herod or Nereus!

Nothing was left to her but ambition which was like the ashes of a dead fire. She seemed driven forward by some remorseless force which refused to let her falter.

Chapter Nineteen

Beside a Well

THE DAY WAS HOT AND SULTRY. NOT A BREATH STIRRED the foliage of the trees that shaded the way through Samaria.

Mara was on her way to Jerusalem. She came at last to the beautiful valley separating the Mountains of Ephraim, at the head of which lay, like a bit of brilliant mosaic set within the green slopes, the little village of Sychar. On the right were the towering peaks of Gerizim, the Mount of Blessings, while from the opposite side, across the sunlit distance, rose the Mount of Curses, grim and forbidding Mount Ebal.

A twisted smile distorted her lips as she looked toward Mount Ebal. Surely God had put His curse upon her! She looked across the sloping stretches of fertile fields with their ripening grain, the shaded spots that marked the orchards with their luscious fruit and the darkening clusters of grapes as they showed against the vivid green of the vineyards in the distance.

Just beyond the roadside was a little thatched hut. A child ran out the door chasing a small scraggly goat. As they ran around the house and out of sight, the echo of the child's laughter came to her. A sigh escaped her. Laughter and happiness! The peace of home! How unspeakably wonderful it must be! She urged her donkey on with a vicious prod of her heel. She could never know peace again.

As she approached the little grove that shaded the well of Jacob, she drew in her reins and prepared to dismount and water her donkey. There were two people at the wellside talking, so she stopped some distance away to wait until they should leave. One of them was a woman and today she lacked the courage to face the woman's cold stare. As she took a closer look at the two her eyes widened with surprise. Sitting there at the wellside talking to the woman was Jesus the Nazarene.

She had heard much about him and had seen him from a distance several times since the encounter on the road outside Jerusalem. He possessed some mysterious power that she couldn't understand. She experienced a strange mingling of emotions whenever she saw him, an infinite yearning which invariably brought the tears to her eyes and left her miserable for days, yet there was a defiant impulse which fought against that yearning and made her hate him.

She wondered what he was doing here talking to this woman. He was a Jew, while the woman was not only a despised Samaritan but an outcast like herself. She had met the woman on one of her visits to Samaria. Experience with the men of her race caused her lip to curl scornfully as she watched him talking to her as if she were a respectable person. This man was a cheat like all the others! What a leader for the children of Israel! They

should see him now! What a rich morsel this would be
for the gossips! Presently, however, her scorn gave way
to doubt, then amazement, for the woman's face revealed strange emotions as the two talked—doubt, wonder, then adoration. The calm majesty of the Nazarene
filled Mara with a feeling of respect which surmounted
her scorn.

Finally the woman turned away and started toward
the village, her face illumined by some inner light which
transfigured it completely. A sob rose in Mara's throat as
she looked at her. There was a look of peace there.
Peace! The word clutched at her heart and wrung it
with longing as the woman came toward her.

The woman was about to pass her without seeing her,
but she stopped her. "What did he tell you to make you
look like that?" she asked breathlessly.

"He told me he was the Messiah! He's the Son of
God!" the woman said tremulously, with a rapturous
look in her eyes.

"Oh, is that all?" Mara replied in disappointment, and
then asked scornfully, "And you're fool enough to believe it, just because he said so?"

"He told me everything I ever did. I'm going to the
village and tell them to come and hear him talk. He's
greater than any prophet who's ever been here. He's
wonderful!"

"Well, it wouldn't take a prophet to tell what you are,"
Mara scoffed. "I thought he'd performed some miracle
or something, by the way you look."

"He has," answered the woman solemnly. "He's given
me a new outlook on life. Everything that's past seems

to have been washed out of my heart. Nothing but a miracle could do that."

"Even the desire to return to your latest lover?" Mara laughed.

"Yes, even that," the woman agreed quietly.

"What will your lover say about it?"

"I don't know. But I'm going to find him and bring him to hear the Master talk. I want him to have the same experience that has come to me. I wish everyone in the village could have the chance to feel as I do."

"How do you feel?" Mara asked with a twisted smile.

"I can't describe it, but since I asked him to give me that strange living water he was talking about, my heart seems filled with a great peace. Somehow the whole world seems different. Nobody but God could do a thing like that."

Mara turned away and a surge of bitterness rushed over her. Peace! This outcast like herself had found it at last. It shone from her eyes, in her transfigured face, in the tones of her voice. Her gaze involuntarily turned to the well curb and the man sitting there. He was looking at her and there was understanding and infinite compassion in his look.

"He's looking at you!" the woman cried, grasping Mara's hand. "Go and talk to him," she urged.

"What could he do for me?" Mara cried in stricken voice.

"He could do the same thing he did for me. Go and talk to him. I can't explain it but he'll make you understand."

"No! No!" Mara cried through pale lips as she turned

away and mounted her donkey, urging the animal to a mad pace down the dusty road.

"Peace! Peace!" she cried in agony. "What peace could he bring me? Nothing but death can ever bring me peace, and there's no hope even then."

Sobbing aloud, heedless that great tears ran down her face and left tiny streaks upon her cheek, heedless of the dust and hot sun, of the parching thirst that made her throat ache and burn, she went on down the long road.

Chapter Twenty

At the Temple

THE TIME OF THE FEAST OF THE TABERNACLES HAD come. The air was crisp with fall. The roads leading to Jerusalem were thronged with caravans of camels and donkeys laden with merchandise. During this festival the merchants from Arabia, Egypt and Rome would reap a rich harvest from the thousands of pilgrims who would flock to the city. There were rich Jews on horseback coming down from Galilee, others less prosperous, on the slow-moving donkeys, still others toiling along the dusty roads on foot, all bound for the massive gates of the Holy City.

Inside the city, crowds were milling about the narrow streets. Droves of cattle and sheep were herded near the Temple and doves in their wicker cages were piled high for the poorer people who could not afford a calf or a sheep.

Booths were erected on the flat roofs and every house was crowded to its utmost long before the first day of the feast. This was no pleasure-mad mob that filled the city, but a mass of devotees obeying the command of the God who had chosen them as His own from the time of faithful Abraham.

Mara entered the city the evening before the feast. She felt more like an outcast than ever on these festival occasions. Her heart yearned more than ever for human companionship and sympathy. At night, when the streets were almost deserted, she slipped down the street that led to Rachel's home and stood there in the darkness, hoping for a sight of Rachel or the sound of her voice.

Once she had seen Rachel coming home and mounting the outer stairway and a sob choked her as she drew back further into the shadows. Did Rachel ever dream of her, she wondered, when she sat there alone in the darkness? Was there any love left in Rachel's heart for the sister who was worse than dead?

One morning, when the feast was at its height, she saw a crowd moving toward the Temple and was drawn into its center before she realized it. They seemed terribly excited and curiosity prompted her to go with them and find the cause.

As they approached the Temple the crowd became more dense. Presently the crowd parted, forming a narrow lane of respectful Jews. A group of Pharisees were entering the Temple courtyard. Mara laughed. Always the same servile respect for these smirking hypocrites! She could tell these fools some things about these holy men with their pious faces and blue-bordered robes!

Following the Pharisees came a group of men dragging a woman. The woman was fighting and cursing her captors in a furious, shrieking voice. Mara caught a glimpse of her face and the mocking smile left her own lips. This woman was a creature like herself. What were they going to do to her?

"What's all the fuss about?" asked a man near her.

"The Pharisees have set a trap for the Nazarene and we're waiting to see the fun," explained someone.

"Where is the Nazarene?" asked the first man.

"He's inside the courtyard. The Pharisees have taken a woman who has broken a commandment of Moses. They are taking her to the Nazarene to see what he will tell them to do with her."

"What can he do? He's no judge," commented someone.

"Of course not. Didn't I say it was a trick? According to the Law of Moses, she should be stoned. The Pharisees want to see whether he will say she should be stoned or if he will want her to go free."

"There's no trick in that. Moses' law hasn't been kept for years."

"That's true. But don't you see how clever the Pharisees are? Even if the Law hasn't been kept it's still being taught to our sons. If the Nazarene says the woman shouldn't be stoned, then all will see for themselves that he doesn't respect the Law of Moses. If he says she ought to be stoned, it'll prove he doesn't practice what he preaches and that this new doctrine of love he's been preaching about is only a trick to attract the people. They've got him in a spot he'll never get out of."

Impelled by some driving force within her which was stronger than mere curiosity, Mara slipped within the court. She had not seen Jesus of Nazareth since that day beside the well. She was glad of that, for her encounters with him had disturbed her. She wanted to see how he would deal with one of her own kind when he was brought face to face with the Mosaic Law. This would be different from that quiet talk with the woman at the well.

Deep within her was the same yearning she had felt that day at Sychar, the same inner cry to some power he possessed which she could not understand, yet longed to know. She hid behind one of the columns where she could see and yet be hidden from the eyes of the mob. She covered her head with the long scarf, hiding the thick braids of her hair, which she wore about her neck. She was close enough to see his face clearly now. He seemed oblivious of the crowd and was tracing letters in the dust. One of the Pharisees was talking to him.

"Master, Moses in the Law commanded that such a creature should be stoned. What do you say?"

As she waited for his answer, her gaze swept over the assembled throng. There were men of every walk in life, from the Pharisee and the Sadducee to the humble cheese-vendor who sat at the market corner. She recognized many of them and longed to tell them what hypocrites they were. She longed to tell this man who was being trapped that they were not worthy to pass judgment upon him or upon this woman who had broken the Law. Her antagonism toward the Nazarene melted away and she felt a measure of sympathy for him. He seemed so alone in that mob with no friendly face near him. Perhaps he, too, knew what it was to be lonely, to have every man's hand against him.

He rose slowly and looked about him. Pity and sadness were in his glance. The Pharisees wore a smile of triumph on their faces. The crowd watched with strained interest.

He looked at them for a time, then said quietly, "He that is without sin among you, let him first cast a stone at her."

Mara could feel the sudden hush fall over the mob like a pall of smoke settling over a sea suddenly becalmed. His voice stirred her to the depths of her being. Tears came and trickled unheeded down her cheek.

Then there was a strange happening. Like the scattering of leaves before the wind, the throng began to diminish. The Pharisees, after an interval of frozen amazement, turned their eyes, now no longer alight with triumph, toward a multitude who had turned their backs upon them and were leaving them to settle this situation as best they could. Realizing that they had been made ridiculous before their people, they finally turned and left the court, muttering furiously to each other.

Mara watched them go and suppressed a desire to give way to hysterical laughter. What a dismal end to their cunningly devised plot! They were fleeing from the trap they themselves had set! Soon there was no one left but the Nazarene and the woman. The woman remained where they had thrown her, in a huddled heap not far from him. All her defiance and rage had left her.

He spoke to her quietly. "Where are your accusers? Has no man condemned you?"

The woman raised her eyes and looked into his face, then dropped them again in unaccustomed humility. "No man, Lord," she murmured.

He answered in a voice full of compassion, and a nameless something which Mara could not understand made her catch her breath with a little sob. "Neither do I condemn you: go, and sin no more," he said.

The woman raised her head in quick surprise. She stared at him in amazed silence, but as his eyes held her gaze, her face became illumined with that same inner light Mara had seen on the face of the woman of Sychar. She uttered a glad cry and bowed her head at the Nazarene's feet. Mara could not hear what he said but the woman rose and left the court with the same buoyant step and transfigured face that Mara had seen before. As she left the court, she covered her head with her scarf and wrapped it about her throat. She was no longer a courtesan!

The Nazarene turned to leave and Mara started impulsively after him. What he had done for those two he could surely do for her! If she were to go on living, something must be done to stop the torturing pain in her heart. She had forgotten Herod, forgotten Judah, forgotten everything but her desire to experience the transfiguring power that this man possessed.

At the gate she stopped, transfixed. Standing just outside, watching the Nazarene with interested gaze, was Mithradas. Though he wore the travel-stained garments of a civilian, she recognized him. Memory returned to her, killing the sudden hope that had brought brief joy now turned bitter. With a loud burst of laughter she tore her veil from her head and ran down the street. Mithradas turned and looked after her, and as he recognized her, there was an expression of amazement and pity on his face.

Chapter Twenty-one

The End of the Road

THE TIME HAD COME FOR MARA TO RETURN TO DECAP-
olis. Laden with bundles and followed by a boy carrying
others, she engaged one of the small boats lying at the
landing in Capernaum.

Since the scene at the Temple, a feeling of desperation had assailed her, a grim determination to put an end
to the life she had been condemned to live. She couldn't
go on.

When the boat landed at the other side, she allowed
the boy to help her carry the provisions up the steep
pathway. Wide-eyed and curious, he left her there and
returned to wait for her at the shore. The girl stored
her packages in the place prepared for them and stood
for a while looking over the rugged hillside. She was
surprised to discover that there was no guard at hand
to see that she did not approach within the forbidden
boundary. Absorbed in her own misery, she had not
noticed that for some time she had not been shadowed
by her own spy.

Herod had withdrawn his soldiers from Decapolis
for two reasons. First, and most important, there was
serious trouble in his affairs. Aretas, king of Arabia

Petraea, the father of the wife Herod had put aside
when he married Herodias, was doing his best to stir
up a revolt in revenge for the insult to his daughter.
He had threatened this when Herod had first banished
his daughter but Herod had not been disturbed by his
threats, for he felt secure in his power and in the hope
of becoming king of Palestine. But the interruption and
delay in his plans left him an easy mark for Aretas and
all his forces were required to subdue the threatened
revolt.

After the novelty had disappeared he had lost interest
in Mara's punishment. The memory of his love for her
still lingered in his heart and at times he still longed
for her, but now he had more pressing interests than
an unfaithful concubine.

Presently Mara saw Judah coming toward her. She
could see that he shivered as the cool wind from the
lake touched his thin body. It seemed almost a miracle
that he had survived this long, exposed as he was to the
elements. Horror and fear swept over her as he drew
nearer. Presently he stopped and stared at her with a
light in his eyes like that of a beast of prey about to
spring on a helpless victim. As she looked at him in
terror he turned abruptly away and started back over
the hill.

An agonized cry tore through her pale lips as he
turned from her with no sign of recognition. Her terror
was forgotten.

"Judah! Judah!" she cried, and in her voice all the
pent-up suffering of the past months found expression.

He turned swiftly and an uncertain light wavered in

his eyes, as if memory were struggling to pierce the fog that clouded his mind. Then he uttered a shrill, unearthly cry and dashed across the rocky space between them, straight toward her.

Swiftly she drew out a little dagger that she had carried for just such an opportunity as this. If he would come close enough, she would plunge the dagger into his heart and then kill herself. Tensely she waited. When he was almost near enough for her to strike, he uttered a wild shriek and began racing around and around in a mad circle; then he fell to the ground, where he lay writhing and foaming in convulsions. With a terrified cry Mara fled from him down toward the boat.

When she was almost there she stopped, panting and spent. What a coward she had been not to have struck when the opportunity had been hers. She would go back and kill him while he lay there, even if the sight of him made her cold and sick with horror. Then she would kill herself. Wearily she returned to where he had fallen, but he had vanished among the rocky caverns.

As she returned to Capernaum, she fought the desire to slip over the side of the boat and sink beneath the blue waters. The sea was quiet and it seemed to whisper to her that there was peace and oblivion beneath its waves. She determined that the next trip to Decapolis would be her last. If Judah were still alive and no other opportunity came to her to kill him, she would kill herself and leave him to his fate. At least she wouldn't be alive to know what that fate might be. This determination brought a small measure of comfort to her and a faint courage to go on for a little longer.

The next two days she spent in Capernaum. Herod's prophecy had come true, for she was so weary of the road that the very thought of going on the ceaseless journeyings sickened her. On the third day she started reluctantly on her way. The city was swarming with life. In the market place late housewives were haggling over the price of fruit and vegetables. Barefooted children were playing in and out among the stalls, calling to one another with shrill voices or whistling on small reed flutes. The smell of fish and over-ripe fruit hung heavy in the air.

Picking his way through the throng, Nereus strode confidently, his short brown mantle swaying gracefully. At a corner he turned and his step became slower; then he stopped and stared in surprise at the man he saw on the opposite side of the street. It was Mithradas. After a cautious glance about him, Nereus approached Mithradas.

"Greetings." He slapped Mithradas upon the back, laughing at Mithradas' start of surprise. "I haven't seen you for ages. What brings you to Capernaum?"

"Don't pretend you don't know. The Governor's business. I'm watching the house of Simon the Pharisee."

"That's what I came to do," commented Nereus. "The Nazarene dines there today; so we're both here on the same mission."

"Yes. Herod's terribly upset over the increasing popularity of this man."

"Herod's a fool. If it wasn't for Herodias I believe he'd take to his heels and run away from the fellow."

"How is everything at the palace?" asked Mithradas.

"Things haven't gone so well. Aretas has been stirring up trouble. Herod has a stupid idea that the gods have forsaken him, and he's terribly worried. He's taken every available soldier and sent them to subdue the threatened revolt. You may know he's afraid when he withdrew the guards stationed in Decapolis and the fellow who's been following Mara."

"I saw Mara down in Jerusalem," Mithradas said. "There was a crowd at the Temple and the Nazarene was there in the court. When the crowd left she came out and she ran out of the court and down the street laughing wildly, as if she were being pursued by demons. But there were tears running down her face. Somehow I felt sorry for her."

Nereus laughed. "What's happened to you to make you so tenderhearted? You haven't fallen under the spell of this castoff of Herod, have you?"

"I can't forget that I was partly to blame for what happened to her."

"Nonsense! You couldn't help obeying orders. If it hadn't been you, it would have been someone else. Herodias was determined to get rid of her."

"I don't blame Herod for being worried about the Nazarene, Nereus. There's some strange power about him that I can't understand."

"What's happened to you? Getting afraid like Herod?" mocked Nereus.

"If you'd heard the Nazarene as often as I have and had seen some of the things he's done, you'd understand what I mean," Mithradas said solemnly.

"The next thing I know you'll be joining this rabble

which follows the Nazarene." Nereus prodded Mithradas playfully.

Just then they saw Mara approaching on her way out of town.

"I wonder if she realizes she's not being followed," said Nereus. "Herod would be amused if he knew she was still obeying his commands even though he's lost interest in her."

Mithradas stared at her with interest. "She's still beautiful," he remarked.

"Did you expect her to lose her beauty the moment she lost Herod's favor?"

Mara didn't see them and would have passed them, but Nereus stopped her. "Greetings, Mara. You look as fresh as if you hadn't traveled a mile in months."

The mockery in his voice brought a tinge of color to her cheek but she would have gone on without answering. Nereus stood in front of her, blocking her path.

"Don't go yet. This is the first chance I've had to talk to you for a long time."

"Let me pass." Her voice was calm but her eyes blazed.

He regarded her with an amused smile. "Still haughty, my queen—even though you've been driven from your kingdom. How's your lover? I hope he hasn't grown tired of you, too."

She drew out her dagger and struck viciously at him. Only his agile leap aside saved him. With a swift and deft movement he caught her wrist and the dagger clattered to the ground.

"It's a good thing I've got a swift pair of feet," he remarked.

"I'm only sorry I wasn't quicker!" she stormed.

"You've become quite a vicious person, Mara."

"You're responsible for what I've become and the next time I won't be so slow," she promised him.

"People have died for what you've done. I warn you that it isn't wise to try to murder a soldier of Rome."

"I'm not afraid of your threats," she cried. "A soldier of Rome! You're a spy and a cheat and a thief! If Herod knew what a loyal soldier you are to him, he'd have you crucified!"

"I ought to kill you for that!" His tones matched hers in anger now. "I've half a mind to do it. You know too much."

"You wouldn't dare! You're too big a coward. You're afraid of Herod. But it's just what I wish you would do. Go ahead and kill me!" Her voice broke suddenly.

A mocking smile twisted Nereus' thin lips. "It would be a pity to kill you and rob your lover of his only means of obtaining food."

Her face went white but she didn't answer him. She turned away and started across the street; then she stopped suddenly and stared past Simon's house. The anger died from her eyes and the bitterness was wiped from her face. "It's the Nazarene!" she murmured.

Mara stood watching as Jesus of Nazareth and a few disciples approached and entered the Pharisee's house. Nereus watched her, amused by her eagerness.

"Why don't you go in and be one of the uninvited guests at the feast?" he asked. "They say he eats with publicans and sinners, so he might not object to your presence."

She paid no attention to him. She seemed to have forgotten Nereus and Mithradas completely.

"I've hated him and I've been afraid of him and I've run away from him, yet he keeps crossing my path," she said half aloud. "Why should I be afraid?" Her voice rose to a despairing wail.

"There's no reason to be afraid of him," Mithradas said, and a note of compassion betrayed itself in his voice. "He has some marvelous power, though, that I can't understand."

She turned to him eagerly. "Have you seen it, too?"

"Yes. Many times."

"Trickery!" scoffed Nereus.

"It isn't trickery," answered Mara, but she wasn't looking at him. Her eyes were fastened upon the house of Simon. She was talking aloud, as if she were without hearers. "It's a miracle—a miracle that brings peace. *Peace!* Oh, I wonder if he could bring peace to me!"

"Not while Herod lives," retorted Nereus.

She ignored his taunt and left them standing there watching her with mingled curiosity and surprise as she approached the house of Simon. Already a group of inquisitive people had gathered about the open door. Mara hesitated a moment, then pushed past them and entered the house. She had eyes for no one but the Nazarene taking his seat upon the low couch on one side of the table at the guest's place.

She seemed drawn to him by some power outside herself. She didn't stop to think of the gravity of her offense in entering the house of this Pharisee nor of the insult her presence was to his guests. She didn't seem to notice

the amazed stares of the group about the door nor hear
their whispers as she crossed the room to where Jesus
was.

Suddenly she realized what she had done, and the
realization paralyzed her. He turned and looked at her;
then she forgot the amazed and horrified stares of Simon
and his guests, for she was looking into the depths of
eyes that held her gaze in spite of her humiliation and
fright. She read there such compassion and such understanding that sudden tears came to her eyes. Those eyes
which seemed to see into her soul told her that he didn't
despise her. The same yearning invitation she had seen
in them at the wellside was there still, calling to something in her which cried out to him in a voiceless yearning.

Impulsively she dropped to his feet and knelt there
as her tears fell faster. Through tear-blurred eyes she
saw that his feet were dusty. Simon had allowed his
guest to sit down to a meal without having had his feet
washed, an unpardonable breach of etiquette. Scarcely
conscious of what she did, she reached within her dress
and drew forth a small alabaster vial of rare perfume. It
was her most costly possession and she had saved it for
an emergency. That morning she had put it there for
safekeeping before she started on her journey. It was the
price of her shame but she didn't think of that now as
she broke the seal and poured its precious contents on
the dust-covered feet. The pungent aroma of the perfume filled the room and as she bowed her head her long
hair swept over the dusty feet and she brushed them
gently as her tears mingled with the perfume. Only her
low sobs broke the silence.

At last the horrified Simon turned to demand that a servant put her out. With a gesture the Nazarene stopped him.

"Simon, I have something to say to you."

Mara's sobs ceased as she listened to his voice, a voice like strange, sweet music.

"Say on, master," said Simon, none too graciously.

"There was a certain creditor which had two debtors: the one owed five hundred pence, and the other fifty. And when they had nothing to pay, he frankly forgave them both. Tell me therefore, which of them will love him most?"

"I suppose he to whom he forgave the most," Simon answered, rather impatiently.

"You have guessed rightly." There was a subtle change in his voice. "Do you see this woman? I entered your house, but you gave Me no water for My feet. But she has washed them with tears and wiped them with her hair. You did not anoint My head as a welcome guest, but she has anointed My feet with ointment. Her sins, which were many, are forgiven."

A heavy silence followed. The guests stared at him while his quiet gaze traveled over them. Then He turned and spoke to Mara.

"Your sins are forgiven."

She raised her eyes, no longer afraid to meet his. By some miracle her heart seemed to have been washed clean. Everything he had seemed to see there before had vanished. There was nothing there now which could not meet his gaze. A great weight seemed lifted from her, and her head whirled with the wonder of the experience. As she stared at him with rapt gaze, she knew. It was peace she felt! *Peace!* Now she understood what had happened to those other two.

She knelt and once more kissed his feet, looked again into the face bent above her and murmured a word of thanks. Then she rose and silently left the room.

As she came out of the house Nereus saw her face, and he stared at her in surprise. Without giving him a glance, utterly oblivious of his existence, she went down the street while she covered her head with her scarf and wrapped it closely beneath her chin.

"What do you make of that?" Nereus asked, puzzled.

"I've seen it happen before, but I can't understand it," replied Mithradas. "It's all a part of this man's strange power."

"It's a good thing for her that Herod has lost interest in her or he'd find out why she covered her head. I'll keep an eye on her. It may be worth while."

"Now you see why I said that Herod has cause to be afraid of the Nazarene," said Mithradas gravely.

Nereus laughed harshly. "Herod has nothing to fear from him."

"Why not?"

"You'll know soon enough." He decided it wouldn't be wise to tell Mithradas that he had just returned from Jerusalem and that what he had done there was eminently satisfactory to Herodias. He had succeeded better than he had hoped in the mission she had entrusted to him. The Pharisees were determined to put Jesus of Nazareth to death.

Chapter Twenty-two

The Dawn of Hope

AFTER THE FIRST THRILL OF EXCITEMENT AND EXALTA-
tion, a frightened, helpless feeling stole over Mara. That
unconscious covering of her head as she left Simon's
house was a symbol to her own soul as well as a sign
to the world that she had left the old life forever. But
there was no place for Mara the Wanderer but the open
road. What would Herod do when he learned what had
happened?

She knew now that she couldn't kill Judah and herself as she had planned. She no longer wanted to die.
The desire for life surged within her more strongly than
ever, but once more the pall of hopelessness hung over
her, banishing her new-found joy. She could see no way
out. What should she do? There was no one to help
her, no one to whom she could turn. Perhaps the Nazarene could help her. She decided to go back to Simon's
house and wait for him to come out, but even as she
started back a sudden thought halted her steps. Nereus
and Mithradas were there watching the house, and they
were Herod's spies. A cold fear seized her as she remembered the Baptist. Nereus and Mithradas must be

175

spying upon the Nazarene. If she went back there, she might bring added danger to him as well as to herself.

Disappointed and dejected, she continued on her way. As she reached the place where she usually kept her donkey, a feeling of desolation swept over her. Mechanically she paid the man for keeping him; then, mounting the donkey, she rode slowly over the highway toward the south. After she had traveled for some distance, she realized for the first time that there was no one following her. What did it mean? Had Herod really withdrawn his guard, or was this a trick of his to lead her into another trap? She had forgotten the guard at Simon's house.

Mara neared Jerusalem and once more there came to her a longing to see Rachel. Perhaps Rachel could tell her what to do. When she reached her destination she still saw no sign of her guard but she feared that she might be followed, so she sought lodging for the night in a distant part of the city and waited until after dark to go to see Rachel.

Her heart throbbed with painful memories as once more she stood at the outer door, knocking. A sleepy porter opened the grill and asked her name. He went grumbling to seek his mistress, leaving her standing there in the darkness. People who wouldn't give their names couldn't be admitted at this hour without orders.

Finally Rachel came to the door.

"It's Mara, Rachel," Mara whispered, as Rachel stared at her through the small grill. "I want to talk to you."

With a glad cry Rachel opened the door and took Mara in her arms.

"It's so good to have someone's arms about me once more." Mara's voice choked with sobs. "You don't know how starved I've been for just a little love, just the touch of someone's hand in friendship! Let's go somewhere where we can talk. I have so much to tell you."

Rachel took her up to the roof and sat beside her under the trellis. Mara told her all that had happened until the moment she had reached Rachel's house.

"I felt somehow that the Master could help you," Rachel said when she had finished. "He's done such wonderful things. I wanted so much to tell you about him but you never came near me," she finished reproachfully.

"I was afraid to and I didn't think you'd want me coming here."

Rachel put her arms about Mara. "I wanted you, no matter what people thought about you. I'm so glad all that's over now. I'm not going to let you leave me again."

"That's what I wanted to talk to you about, Rachel. I'm still Herod's slave and still under his sentence. What do you suppose he'll do when he finds out what's happened?"

"You won't have to be afraid of him much longer," Rachel assured her. "Jesus of Nazareth is our promised Messiah. He'll deliver us soon from Roman rule."

"Do you really think he is the Messiah?" There was a new note of hope in Mara's voice.

"I know he is. I've heard him preach and I've seen the miracles he's performed." She lowered her voice. "It's whispered that the time is at hand. You have no idea how eagerly the people are waiting for him. Some-

times I get so excited, thinking about what it will mean
for our country to be once more the glorious land it was
in the days of Solomon!"

"Why couldn't he have come just a little sooner, before Judah lost his reason!" Mara's voice broke.

"Mara!" cried Rachel excitedly. "I believe he could
cure Judah. I'm sure he could! Why didn't I think of it
before?"

"Do you really think he could?" Mara asked eagerly.
She would not let herself hope, yet Rachel's excitement was contagious.

"I saw him cure a man who was born blind and they
say he brought a little girl back to life. Surely if he can
do things like that, he can cure Judah."

"Oh, if only he could! How shall I go about asking
him if he can?"

"Stay here with me and wait until he returns. He'll
come again soon, I'm sure. Then we can ask him."

"I can't do that. I couldn't sit here waiting day after
day for him to come. Judah might die while I sat here
doing nothing. I know what I'll do! I'll go and look for
him myself. O Rachel! Think what it will mean if he can
cure Judah!"

"I heard him say one day that all things were possible
to one who believed," Rachel told her.

"I shall make myself believe!" Mara cried.

"Stay here tonight," Rachel urged.

"I'd love to, but I'm afraid. I don't want to bring
trouble to you. I'll leave early in the morning for Galilee
and I'll come back as soon as I can after I've found
him."

"Have you enough money?" Rachel asked anxiously.

"Oh, I'd forgotten about that! I have only a little left."

"Wait and I'll get you some." She went downstairs and returned in a few minutes with the money.

"This is all I have in the house. When that is gone, you know where to come for more," she said as she gave it to Mara.

She followed Mara to the stairway, held her in her arms, then kissed her tenderly. "I shall go to the Temple every day and pray that you will find him and that he can heal Judah," she said.

"Pray that the Messiah will soon be on his throne, before Herod has a chance to find out about me," Mara begged, kissing her and slipping out into the night.

Chapter Twenty-three

The Last Journey

MARA CLIMBED THE RUGGED SLOPE AND STOOD PANTING at the top of the hill. She put her packages in the place where she was accustomed to leave them, then sat down on a boulder to rest. There was no one in sight and no sound broke the deathly silence.

Fear clutched her heart. If there were no guards here in Decapolis, then Judah must be dead. Perhaps they had come back and found him dead on that terrible day when she had seen him writhing in convulsions. That must have been the end of this horrible nightmare, but though she had hoped for this end, she felt suddenly desolate, forsaken and frustrated.

The girl had started her search for the Nazarene with such high hopes, such eager anticipation that she had refused to be daunted by the failure which continually met her efforts to find him. Day after day she followed him as he eluded her like some will-o'-the-wisp. Everywhere she heard of the wonderful cures he had performed, of the strange new doctrine he preached, yet she was never able to find him.

As time passed, her anxiety grew, for there was al-

181

ways hanging over her the fear that Herod would seize
her or that Judah would die or be put to some further
torture.

At last the time came for her to go to Decapolis again.
Her money was almost gone but she couldn't return to
Jerusalem for she was afraid to wait longer than the
appointed time. When she reached Capernaum she
heard that Jesus had been preaching not far from there.
Some said he had left the night before for the other
side of the lake. She had no time to investigate those
rumors until her return from Decapolis. She bought
what supplies she could and started on her trip across
the lake. Now Judah was gone and her hopes had ended.
She rose with a sigh of resignation and drew her mantle
more closely about her. The night before there had been
one of the sudden storms which were so frequent on the
lake at this time of the year, and a chill, cutting wind
blew across the hills. Perhaps someone in Gadara might
be able to tell her what had become of Judah. It was
only a faint hope but she couldn't leave without trying to find out if anyone knew what had become of
him.

Perhaps Herod had taken him away and put him to
torture. Perhaps Nereus had told him what had happened that day at Simon's house. Fear hastened her
steps over the rocky path that led down through the
little valley to the higher hills beyond.

As she reached the top of the hill she could see the
shore that lay in front of the village. A crowd was
gathered there. She could hear the echo of their excited
voices. There seemed to be an argument about some-

thing, for they were gesturing wildly and pointing to the lake. There was a small boat beached near by.

While she watched them a group of men left the crowd and got into the boat. It was pushed out from the shore and then she recognized one of the men in it. It was Jesus of Nazareth. A heartbroken cry escaped her. She had found him at last and now it was too late! He was there and he was leaving before she could get to him. But Judah had disappeared and it wouldn't matter now, even if she could get to him in time to speak to him. The disappointment and utter hopelessness which swept over her were more than she could bear. She sat down on the hillside and sobbed.

After the storm of tears had passed, she wiped her eyes and started once more for the village. The crowd had scattered and there was only one man left on the shore. He was looking out toward the boat which was disappearing in the distance. At her approach he turned and faced her. It was Judah.

She caught her breath with a sharp cry of amazement. Her heart seemed to stop beating and everything swam before her eyes. Then the hills echoed to her cry of rapture.

"Judah! Judah!"

He stood staring at her.

"Oh, is it really you, Judah?" Her voice was fearful, as if she still couldn't believe her eyes. "You've been cured!" she cried as she advanced toward him. "The Nazarene has cured you!"

"Yes," he answered slowly.

She couldn't take her eyes off his face. All the loathsomeness of filth and matted hair and scarred, bleeding skin had vanished. He was the same boy she had seen first outside the Jerusalem gate, strong, handsome.

"It's too wonderful to believe!" she exclaimed. "I've looked for him for so long to ask him to cure you and today when I came here and couldn't find you I thought you were dead. Oh, I'm so glad, Judah, that all the horror is gone and you're yourself again. I just can't believe it! It's so wonderful! So wonderful!"

She became aware at last of his silence, of the coldness in his eyes, the unsmiling lips which made his face seem stern and hostile. This was no glad reunion. He had not taken her in his arms as she had pictured so often in her days of weary searching for the Nazarene. There was no kiss to welcome her. She had forgotten the past, everything but that he was here, that his reason had been restored, that all the longing of the weary months was ended.

The smile left her face and her eyes were clouded with hurt surprise. "You—you—aren't glad to see me," she faltered.

"Why should I be glad to see Herod's concubine?" he asked coldly.

"Oh!" she exclaimed through trembling lips, and the word was a cry of agony.

"I can't forget that scene in the torture chamber, Mara," Judah's voice continued, cold and stern and harsh. "I can't forget the time when I learned that the girl I had loved and admired was nothing but the plaything of Herod. That's the one memory that remained with me when everything else left me. It's tortured me all these months."

He spoke slowly and bitterly and it seemed to her that the lines of suffering she had seen on his face that day in the torture chamber returned, etched more deeply.

"I had forgotten you'd still remember that," she stammered. "I had almost forgotten what happened that day. So much has happened since then." She was fighting tears.

"What happened after I saw the Baptist's head? I thought Herod was going to kill us both. I was hoping he would!"

"He had planned to kill us, but you became a raving madman and he was afraid to kill you. Death would have been too merciful for me so he planned something worse."

Her voice faltered. She had never in the darkest hour of the past months pictured a time like this, when she would have to face the agony of his scorn a second time.

"What did he do to you?" he asked dully, without interest.

She raised her eyes entreatingly to his probing gaze, then dropped them again before the cold, accusing light in his eyes.

"You may as well know the whole truth," she said at last, resignedly. "Herod sent me out to sell myself on the highways, for the money that would buy your food."

"And you went?"

"Yes. I had to. O Judah, I tried not to! But there was no way out. Surely you know Herod and you should realize that there was no escape from his vengeance."

"You could have died!" he cried harshly.

She failed to observe the suffering which brought that harsh note to his voice. She heard only the harshness, falling like the stroke of a lash upon her heart.

"Death would have been most welcome, Judah," she replied sadly. "How glad I would have been to die! But it was you who kept me alive, you who kept me going when I felt that I just couldn't go on. I longed to drive a dagger through my heart, but the thought of you here and of what I had brought to you and of the torture Herod threatened to make you endure if I failed to obey him kept me from doing it. It was when I thought of you and what I had done to you that a thousand devils seemed to take possession of me and I seemed driven on by them."

In a halting, choking voice, she told him the whole story, not sparing herself, for she felt that nothing she could say would make him despise her any more than he already did. When she told him of her experience at Simon's house, her voice rang with a new note and her face became suddenly radiant, but Judah's face did not reflect the radiance. He said nothing for a while, only stared at her solemnly.

"So they call you Mara the Wanderer, the most notorious courtesan in Palestine," he finally remarked, and there was an added tinge of bitterness in his voice.

"O Judah! Is that all you can say?"

"What else is there to say?"

She approached a little closer and raised her tear-stained face to his.

"Haven't you any love left in your heart for me,

Judah? I loved you so much that I couldn't kill myself and leave you to suffer more. I didn't care what happened to me. It was you alone who mattered. How gladly I would have died for you! I sold my soul for you, Judah. Don't you love me even a little?"

"I loved you when I thought you were something lovely and unapproachable." A spasm of pain crossed his face. "A pure lily—do you remember?"

She shrank from him and turned her face away as a sob rose in her throat.

"Could there be any real love when not even respect remains?"

His voice was thick and strained with grief but to her ears it sounded strange and harsh and she missed the note of suffering.

"I understand," she said wearily. "You despise me. But you don't understand at all, Judah. My life is different now. The past has been wiped out. I'm a different person from what I was then. I'm what you once thought I was. Won't you believe me?"

"In the eyes of the world you'll always be Mara the Wanderer," he stated uncompromisingly.

"Will you always be the madman of Decapolis?" she flashed.

"No. Of course not. I'm no longer possessed of demons. I've been healed."

"Then why not believe that I can be different since I've been healed? Isn't sin a disease of the soul, just as madness is a disease of the mind? If Jesus can cure one, why can't he cure the other?"

"I don't know," he replied disconsolately.

"I'm afraid you don't want to know, Judah."

"Yes, I do. But a faith once shattered is hard to restore and my faith was destroyed that day in Herod's torture room."

After a moment's silence she said quietly, "I've said all there is to say. I suppose I'd better be going."

He was silent and refused to meet her eyes as she stood waiting and hoping for him to speak.

"Good-bye, Judah," she murmured.

"Good-bye." His voice was muffled and choked but she didn't notice.

Mara turned and walked slowly back up the rugged slope, her shoulders drooping wearily. It was over— the dreams, the longing, the hope, the ceaseless searching, the wild fear and despair. Everything was over now. Life stretched before her like a long, dreary road. There was no bitterness in her heart toward him for his self-righteousness, no impatience that he could not believe what she felt in her own heart, only an emptiness, a longing that would never be satisfied, a yearning that she might reach within his heart and open the little door of understanding and love for her which his own suffering had closed against her.

She toiled up the slope, her feet like lead, her body aching with a weariness greater than mere physical exhaustion. Suddenly she heard his voice raised in an agonized cry.

"Mara! Mara!"

He was coming up the slope after her, his face pale and drawn, his lips trembling, his eyes brimming with tears.

"What is it?" she asked quietly, as he came near.

She could feel calm and quiet now for doubt and fear and shame were gone and the certainty of emptiness alone remained.

"I can't let you go! I can't!" he cried breathlessly.

"Why should you want me to stay? You have no faith in me. You have nothing but contempt for me."

"I love you!" he cried. "Nothing matters but that! I've tried to make you believe I didn't and I've tried to make myself believe I didn't, but I do! I do! I love you! Nothing has been able to destroy that. It will always be in my heart."

She advanced toward him with uncertain, faltering step. "Are you quite, quite sure?" she asked tremulously, afraid to let hope rise again.

"Quite, quite sure." He held out his arms to her as a smile spread across his face, wiping out all the bitterness.

At last the dream had come true, but she hesitated, afraid to let herself believe that it was real. "But the past is still in your memory, Judah," she reminded him gravely.

"Yes, it is," he admitted, "and I won't deny that there may be times when it will rise to torture me. But we'll both try to forget, my dearest, and if we're together, nothing else will matter. I love you! I love you!" He took her into his arms.

She put her head on his shoulder with a little sigh of weariness and contentment. "I never thought I'd ever be here again," she murmured.

"Nothing shall ever take you away from me again," he whispered, with his cheek against hers.

"Nothing! Nothing!" she echoed, happy at last with a strange new joy that made her almost afraid, a joy that wiped out the memory of the long months of suffering and bitterness, the memory of everything but that once more his love was hers and that she was safe within the shelter of his arms.

Chapter Twenty-four

Shattered Dreams

JUDAH AND MARA SAT ON THE SLOPE OF THE HILL AND talked, heedless of passing time, but as the shadows began to lengthen, Mara suddenly remembered that the boat was waiting for her at the shore. Everything came back to her with a rude shock. Even though Judah had been restored to sanity, they were both under Herod's sentence. If they returned to Galilee, they would be hunted creatures, afraid of every strange face.

"What are we going to do?" she asked in dismay.

"We'll stay here until the Nazarene returns. I begged him to take me with him but he told me to stay here and tell these people what he had done for me. I'll be glad to do it but it may not be an easy task."

"Why will it be so hard?" she asked.

"Because so many of the villagers will be furious with me. It seems that when Jesus cured me, a great herd of swine suddenly went wild and ran off that steep cliff over there into the lake. They blamed Jesus for it. They said the devils had gone out of me into the swine. Their owners raised a terrible commotion and asked him to leave the village."

"Perhaps we shouldn't stay here." Mara knew from bitter experience what it meant to find every door closed against her.

"I must stay here. I want these people to know about Jesus. Besides, he told me to. I'll make them listen to me and when he goes to Jerusalem to take his throne, I'll join his army and help drive the Romans out. Let's go and see if we can find someone to take us in for the night. Tomorrow we can decide what to do, but I'm never going to let you get out of my sight again." His arm closed about her more tightly.

Mara went down and paid the boatman and in the gathering dusk they entered Gadara. A curious, hostile crowd gathered about them and Mara breathed a prayer of thanksgiving that no one seemed to recognize her.

The owners of the swine threatened to throw him into the lake if he didn't leave at once, but he begged for a chance to tell his story. As he began to tell them about himself, of how he had followed the Baptist and of the miracle which had cured him, they finally gave him a grudging attention. There were some in the crowd who had seen other miracles performed by Jesus and who had heard him preach over in Capernaum and their interest in his story grew. When he had finished speaking and the crowd began to disperse, an old man approached him from the edge of the crowd.

"Come with me, lad," he said. "My name is Nathan. This is my wife, Martha. We'll give you and your wife shelter for the night."

Judah shrank from revealing even a part of the truth

about Mara. As they went toward the little thatched cottage where the old couple lived, Nathan spoke. "I've prayed to live to see such a sight as I saw today," he said. "Now that these old eyes have seen the King again, I'm content to die."

"Then you believe that Jesus is the Messiah?" Judah asked eagerly.

"Indeed I do. Who else could speak a word and heal a madman as he did? I've heard of him and the miracles he performed and I longed to see him, but I never thought I would. Martha and I are too old to travel about much, but I've been hoping he'd come here."

They reached the house and went inside and while Martha busied herself with preparation for the meal, Mara and Judah sat and listened to the old man talk.

"I've been waiting all my life to see the King again. I saw him once long ago. I lived in Bethlehem when he was born. I'll never forget the night the shepherds came to the village saying they had come to see the king of the Jews. One of those shepherds was Benjamin, a friend of mine. He said they had seen a vision of angels out there in the field. Not long after that some men came from the East and brought presents to the child. That's over thirty years ago."

His eyes grew dreamy and his voice grew lower as he remembered the past. "I remember how excited I was when they came. I had never seen anyone like them. They must have been wealthy for their clothes were of the finest silk and their camels had silk trappings. That was perhaps a year after the shepherds came looking for the baby."

"When did you see him?" asked Mara.

"That was when his parents were taking him down to Jerusalem to the Temple. Benjamin was with me as we watched them go. It was the hope of Benjamin's life to live to see him claim his throne."

"Is Benjamin still alive?" asked Judah.

"No. He died years ago, before I left Bethlehem. But I've never stopped looking for him. And now I've seen him!" There was a glow of happiness in his dim eyes.

"He's coming back here again," Judah said. "The time must be near at hand for him to take his throne."

"God grant that it is at hand," ejaculated Nathan fervently.

Mara's heart echoed the prayer.

Judah finally told Nathan a part of the truth about himself and Mara. He believed that their secret would be safe with him.

They sat down to the simple meal of goat's milk, brown bread and cold vegetables. Reverently the two men recited the creed when the meal was finished and then Nathan returned thanks. They sat talking far into the night, of the hope that was so strong within them, of the future which seemed so bright; then Martha took Mara to a tiny room near hers, containing a single narrow cot and a chest. She fixed a pallet for Judah in the main room of the house, a combination of living room, dining room and kitchen.

The next day Judah faced the problem of their immediate future. Nathan urged them to remain with him. He had a little shop near his home where he mended sails and resoled sandals. He insisted that Judah would be a help to him with his work. Judah gratefully accepted his offer. Mara insisted upon taking over the burden of the housework and chattered happily to Martha as she busied herself with pots and dishes, her round white arms bared as she worked a batch of dough or polished the copper pots.

Even though they were living in the shadow of death, they did not let this thought mar the perfect joy of the quiet days. It was so much more than Mara had ever hoped to have, to have Judah near. She refused to let thoughts of Herod mar this joy.

At times, if a stranger passed through the village and happened to look at her with lingering gaze, a sudden fear would seize her and she would think of Herod's spies and wonder if they were looking for her.

Herod was in Jerusalem and was too occupied with other affairs to bother about Judah and Mara. He had entered the city, to the annoyance of his old enemy, Pontius Pilate. Herodias had urged him to go. From the reports Nereus had given her, she thought it wise for them to be on hand to see that her well-laid plans were not bungled. She found to her satisfaction that the Pharisees were eager and anxious to put Jesus of Nazareth to death, but they feared the effect of his death on the populace. She was determined that their fears should not hinder them.

The time of the Passover drew near. In the hearts of the followers of Jesus there was an eager expectancy, a hope that grew with the passing days. When he began his journey south, the news spread like wildfire that he was going down to take the throne, and wherever he went, throngs greeted him and an ever-increasing number followed him.

He came again to Gadara and Judah experienced a warm feeling of satisfaction when he observed that the villagers now welcomed him eagerly. They listened to him preach and brought their sick and crippled for him to heal.

When he left the village on his southward journey, Mara and Judah said good-bye to Nathan and Martha and joined the throng which was marching to the Holy City. Excitement and hope thrilled them. They didn't mind the rocky road or the hot sun or the bitter winds at evening, and when Jerusalem came into view at last, the throng with one accord began to sing that ancient chant, "Hosannah to the Son of David!"

Palm branches were torn from the trees that lined the wayside and were strewn along the path that led through the gate, while many seized them and waved them excitedly at the passing procession.

It seemed to Mara as she walked along with her hand in Judah's firm clasp that her heart would burst with happiness and excitement. At last the dream was about to be realized, the dream of freedom for herself, of freedom for the people of whom at last she felt a part. She was no longer an alien, an outcast, but one of them. Together they would share the glory of this kingdom which had been foretold for so long by their prophets.

That night she and Judah went to Rachel's home. This time they went openly, no longer afraid of Herod, for they were confident that Herod would soon be flee-

ing for his life. The little group sat talking far into the
night, of all that had passed and of all for which they
waited so eagerly.

The next few days were spent in a fever of excitement,
expectancy and hope. Then came the appalling news
which struck its crushing blow to dreams and hopes and
plans, that Jesus had been taken prisoner in Gethsemane
and was to be tried for his life.

Joining a group of excited followers, Mara and Judah
hastened to the palace of the High Priest where Jesus
had been taken. A pale, cold moon shone upon them as
they hurried down the street and stood outside with the
crowd gathered there.

While the Sanhedrin was in session Judah told her he
was going to try to raise a volunteer army to storm the
High Priest's palace and rescue Jesus before they passed
sentence upon him.

"It won't do any good," she protested. "You'll only
make it more dangerous for yourself."

"What do I care for myself, if I can free him?" Judah
cried. "If I can get only a few who are not afraid to risk
their lives, we can surprise the guard and get him out of
there before they realize what's going on."

"They'd only arrest him again."

"No, they wouldn't. We wouldn't give them a chance.
Once he is free again, the people will rally round him
and we'd take the kingdom."

"It seems to me that if he wanted to he could perform
some miracle and escape. He doesn't seem to want to be
free."

"Perhaps he would want to be free if he knew his followers were still loyal. When he was arrested in Geth-semane, all of them ran away and left him."

Mara waited anxiously as the hours passed, heedless of chilling winds or tired body, until at last Judah returned, exhausted and defeated.

"It's no use," he said dejectedly. "I couldn't find a handful who were still willing to take a chance with me. The fear of Rome has made cowards of them all."

"And yet you have more to fear from Rome than any of them," she commented.

"But I have more to thank him for," he replied slowly.

The next morning they joined the throng which followed Jesus to the judgment court of Pilate. Mara's feet felt like lead and her heart quivered with a throbbing pain. She had heard from someone who had been in the inner court what the judgment of the Sanhedrin was, but she refused to abandon hope. She was still looking for some miracle to save him. Surely the man who had raised the dead and healed the blind could deliver himself from this Gentile judge! But a fear, a premonition, came to kill that hope. He didn't seem to want to be free! He seemed to be going willingly to a fate he expected. Why was he? How could he be willing?

She saw him at last when they brought him from Pilate's palace, a bleeding victim of a cruel scourging. She knew from experience how he had suffered. Yet he was still majestic, still calm and commanding, though he tottered from physical weakness. Numbly she followed with Judah to the palace of Asmoneus where he was to stand trial before Herod. Hope died within her as she learned that Herod was to be his judge. Back of Herod would be Herodias, and the memory of John the Baptist sickened her with fear. Herod came out upon the balcony overlooking the courtyard to see the prisoner and for the first time since that morning he had sentenced her she saw him. He had changed much in the months that had passed. His face was heavy and sodden. His eyes were bloodshot and the confident look had vanished, leaving them filled with a nameless fear.

What happened after Herod had tired of questioning the prisoner seemed like a horrible nightmare that ended in the slow journey through the narrow streets and out the gate to Golgotha. What a contrast this journey was to his triumphal entry into the city! In through one gate as a conquering king—out through another to be crucified! Side by side, pushed along by the crowd, Mara and Judah went toward Golgotha. As they neared the hill they became separated, but she had forgotten Judah. Nothing seemed to matter now but that figure hanging there outlined against a darkening sky. He who had spoken to her and given her peace and had cleansed her life, was suffering unspeakable agony. A numbness seized her that deadened the tortured ache of her heart. Tears ran down her cheeks and sobs shook her convulsively, but she was scarcely conscious of them, as darkness descended upon the scene, blotting out that suffering form upon the Cross.

The darkness increased and the crowd became suddenly quiet, silenced by fear. Time ceased to exist for Mara until, in the stillness, she heard once more the sound of his voice, that voice which had sounded like strange sweet music in her ears, that marvelous voice that had spoken to her and brought peace to her soul.

"It is finished!"

It was a cry of triumph. How strange and yet how marvelous! It wasn't the faint gasp of a dying man. It seemed incredible, but those words sounded like the shout of victory, the victory of a king who had overcome the last foe and was entering the gates of his kingdom. She strained her eyes in the darkness as she longed for one more glimpse of the face that had become so dear, but tears blinded her eyes so that she could not see, and sobs shook her as the earth trembled and swayed beneath her. The milling throngs, so suddenly silent, fled in terrified disorder, stumbling over one another, leaving Mara alone near the Cross.

Chapter Twenty-five

Despair

IN THE EARLY AFTERNOON MARA AND JUDAH SAT ON THE housetop of Rachel's house. The sun shone as serenely as if nothing had happened to destroy the peace of thousands, as if no tragedy had occurred to banish the hope of a downtrodden nation.

During the hours since the execution on Golgotha, the followers of Jesus had sat in silent groups, too stunned to talk of what had happened. If the leader whom they had believed to be their Messiah could suffer death, they dared not think of what might happen to them. The vision of glory which had dazzled them had faded and nothing was left but the bleakness of despair.

Mara's despair had passed beyond words and she seemed unable to comprehend, in its fullness, the tragedy that had happened. They sat there for a long time without saying a word. She knew what Judah was thinking, and she shrank from opening the old wounds, yet, as the moments passed, she felt that the situation should be discussed and settled now.

"You haven't said a word in ages," she remarked. "Tell me what you're thinking about."

"The same thing we've all been thinking," he answered gloomily. "I'm thinking of the kingdom we hoped for and that will never be. All our dreams and plans are shattered."

He was silent again, staring ahead of him, down the narrow street. The tapping of a cane along the rough stones told them that a blind beggar was passing below. His pitiful call for alms smote Mara with a new stab of pain. A call in the dark! And there was no one to answer that call, no miracle worker to give him hope of release! How like that beggar they were now! In the dark, with no hope!

Judah's harsh laugh broke the silence. "Weren't we foolish to think anyone could conquer Rome? But he was so different from anyone else it's no wonder we all believed he could."

"Perhaps we were all wrong about him, Judah. I've been thinking of all I heard him say in those last days he was alive. We were so intent upon our own selfish ambitions that not one of us really tried to understand what he told us over and over again."

"He admitted that he was the Messiah. At least he didn't deny it when we called him that."

"I know. But he also said, 'My kingdom is not of this world.' I couldn't understand what he meant then. I was thinking too much about the time when Herod would be driven from the land and our own dreams would come true."

"How could we help believing what we did when he entered the city like a king riding to victory? I expected him to go that very day and drive Pilate out."

"Yes, so did I," she agreed, "and I wondered that night, when I was so excited I couldn't sleep, why he hadn't done it. But since it's all over, I've thought more about what he said and I've remembered how sad he looked that day. He didn't look like a conquering king. His face was the saddest I ever saw. Something he said back there in Gadara makes me think perhaps the kingdom he was talking about wasn't an earthly one at all. Perhaps he meant some kind of spiritual kingdom."

"No matter what kind of kingdom he was trying to establish, he's dead and in a borrowed grave," he exclaimed bitterly. "No king would have died like that."

"He must have been willing to die," she argued, "or he would never have hung there all that terrible afternoon in such agony. I believe he could have come down from that cross if he had wanted to. Don't you remember what he said on the way to Jericho? He said he was to give his life as ransom for many."

"Yes, I remember. But I thought he was talking about the service he would render our nation when he became king. How could his death bring a ransom to anyone?"

"I don't know. It's all beyond me." She sighed. "But I keep remembering those last words he uttered on the Cross. It was a shout of victory, Judah! I can't understand it. I seem to be groping in the dark for something I can't quite find, but I have a feeling that some day I shall know the answer."

"I'm groping in the dark, too, and I don't feel there is any answer," he replied bitterly.

"Judah, I know what's the matter with you. You're

thinking about me. You're letting the past come up to torment you."

"Yes, I am," he admitted, looking at her with stricken, tortured gaze. "I've been thinking about it every minute since they crucified him."

Impulsively she laid her hand on his but he failed to respond to the timid caress.

"How quickly you have forgotten your determination to let the past be buried."

"Determination weakens in the face of what has happened, Mara." His voice was grave and tense. "The Nazarene can't be the Son of God. God wouldn't let a Roman ruler put His own Son to death. If he's not the Son of God, then he didn't have the power to forgive your sins."

"I understand what you mean," she said in a muffled voice.

"You're still Mara the Wanderer, the castoff concubine of Herod." Selfish in his own suffering, he was unmindful of the cruelty of his words.

She turned and faced him and spoke in calm, firm tones. "No, Judah, I'm not still Mara the Wanderer. Whether you believe it or not, whether I understand it or not, I'm not the same person I was before he told me my sins were forgiven. Something entered my heart then that nothing can take away. To me, he's still the Son of God, and I shall always worship him because he's given me something no one but God Himself could have given."

He stared at her for a moment, then turned his eyes wearily away.

"I wish I could feel that way about it. But I can't. I just can't."

"You still believe in the miracle that cured you, don't you?"

"Yes, of course. I'm still sane, at least."

"Then why can't you believe in the one that cleansed my heart and life?" she persisted.

"There's a difference. Mine was of the mind. Yours was of the spirit, something that touched your personality more deeply. There's not a man in Judea who would believe you are any different. They'd always look upon you as an outcast."

"Oh, you self-righteous men!" she exclaimed bitterly. "So willing to forget whatever your own past might have held, yet never willing to forgive or forget anything in a woman's life! Heroes who can do no wrong! Yet when Jesus was taken by his enemies, every man fled from him and it was the women who remained with him until the end." She turned from him and stood staring over the city. Then she spoke in a tired, slow voice. "Perhaps it was because we had been forgiven so much that we loved him, so we were not afraid to die with him."

He turned toward her appealingly. "I'm not trying to be self-righteous, Mara. I want to believe as you do. Help me to believe, my dear!" His voice broke suddenly.

She laid her hand on his bowed head with a gentle maternal gesture. "That is something you will have to do for yourself, Judah. No one can help you do it."

He drew her to him desperately and put his head against her shoulder.

"I love you, Mara!" he cried. "No matter what I may

think or believe. We shall be married and go far away
from Jerusalem and I'll make you believe that I have
faith in you, no matter what others may think."

"We can't do that," she informed him as she withdrew
herself from his arms.

"Why not? Are you afraid to trust me after all these
doubts I've expressed?"

"I can never marry anyone. I'm still Herod's slave,"
she reminded him.

"Oh, I'd forgotten that!" he cried in dismay. "And
you're still under his sentence."

"Yes. And I suppose that now he'll kill me."

"We'll have to get away, Mara!" he cried. "Out of the
country and away from Herod's reach."

"We could never get away together, but you must go
at once. I don't want to drag you into any more danger
on my account and he may arrest you again, if you stay
here in Jerusalem."

"You know I wouldn't go away and leave you here.
You've got to get away. We can't just sit here and wait
for him to arrest you."

"I don't want to, but I just can't seem to think," she
said wearily.

"Herod's in Jerusalem, Mara! I'd forgotten that!"

"Yes, I know. But no matter where he is, if he wants to
find me, he'll do it. After all, what difference does it
make? It doesn't matter very much—now—what happens to me."

He caught her to him and kissed her swiftly. "Don't
talk like that! Please don't! I love you! Doesn't that
matter?"

There were tears in her eyes as she answered, "What was it you said that day in Decapolis? 'Could there be any real love when not even respect remains?'"

"I deserve that but it hurts just the same," he said gravely, "and I wish you'd try to forget it."

"We never can forget, Judah. And as long as you feel the way you do, that past would always stand between us."

Rachel's excited voice interrupted them. "Have you heard the news?" she called as she came toward them. "Jesus has risen from the dead!"

They stared at her with wide eyes and parted lips; then Judah ejaculated, in amazement and unbelief, "How do you know?"

"I've been talking to one of the women who saw him with her own eyes. She said they were going to Joseph's tomb to anoint his body with spices. When they reached the tomb the stone was rolled away and there were two angels there. One of them said Jesus was risen from the dead, but they were so frightened they ran away without waiting to hear any more. As they were running away they saw Jesus there in the pathway and he spoke to them."

"Are they sure it really was Jesus?" asked Mara.

"Of course! Two of his disciples went to the tomb and saw the angels and the graveclothes lying in the tomb. Everyone's so excited about it!"

"O Judah!" Mara cried, turning to him with glowing eyes. "Think what this may mean!"

"Perhaps he's coming back from the dead to take his throne and show these Romans that not even death can defeat him," Judah replied.

Mara's face was radiant. "Perhaps that was the meaning of that cry from the cross! O Judah, if he's risen from the dead, you really know that he is the Son of God."

"Yes, he must be. What a poor doubting fool I've been!" he exclaimed contritely.

Rachel left them to go and tell the glad news to Samuel while Mara and Judah sat talking with growing hope of what this resurrection would mean to their hope and to the hope of their people. Presently their conversation was interrupted by the sound of heavy feet mounting the outer stairs and they turned to see who was coming. Mara's eyes widened with fear as the plumed top of a Roman helmet appeared above the balustrade. Her heart almost stopped beating when she saw the face of Nereus beneath the helmet.

He advanced toward them with his customary swagger. A cynical smile hovered about his lips as he looked at the little group standing silently watching him, for Rachel had just returned to join them. He bowed with exaggerated deference to Mara and there was mockery in his voice as he spoke.

"So we meet again—my queen," he greeted her, while a twisted smile flitted across his thin lips.

"What do you want?" demanded Judah, stepping between them with a gesture of defense which brought a short laugh from Nereus.

"I've come to invite both of you to go with me on a little journey to Tiberias. In the dungeon there, there are two cells, one waiting for you and the other for Herod's discarded concubine."

He brushed Judah aside and addressed Mara. "The

last time I talked to you, you tried to stab me," he reminded her. "If you had been a little more kind to me when you were Herod's favorite, perhaps Herod might not have been reminded that you were still alive and no longer obeying his orders. But you despised a humble palace guard when you had the tetrarch's love. That's why Herod has been reminded about you. Remember that in the long days ahead of you."

"Let her alone!" Judah cried, stepping between them again. "Do your talking to me."

"Anything to be accommodating." Nereus laughed, shrugging his shoulders. "But let's do our talking on the way to Galilee."

He called a crisp order and two soldiers appeared at the top of the stairway.

Rachel threw her arms about Mara and cried frantically, "They can't take you away from me like this! They can't!"

Mara gently disengaged herself from Rachel's arms. "There, there, Rachel dear, don't cry. Think of Samuel and the children," she whispered. "Don't do anything that will bring trouble to them."

She turned to Judah and murmured, "O Judah! I'm so sorry that I've brought you to this. I never dreamed that this would be the end of all our hopes and plans."

"What does it matter, so long as we're together?" he whispered as he put his arm about her.

They walked down the steps, with a soldier on each side and Nereus following. A smile of amusement was still on his dark face.

Chapter Twenty-six

An Unwelcome Conference

Visitors swarmed into the city of Tiberias. They came on foot, on horseback, and on swift, lumbering camels. It was a noticeable fact that few of them were Jews. They were Romans of every class, Arab sheiks with their followers in soiled burnouses and turbans much the worse for wear, Egyptians moving leisurely and quietly, in marked contrast to the noisy men from the near-by desert.

All of them were going toward the new amphitheater which Herod was to dedicate with the largest birthday celebration he had ever had. The amphitheater, with its columned archways, rose tier on tier above the sand-covered arena. A constant stream of people drifted through the gates and though the hour was early, the seats in the lower tiers were filling fast.

Mithradas was stationed at the main gateway of the amphitheater. With alert gaze he watched the crowds. They gathered in groups about the lists posted on each side of the gateway, announcing in Latin, Greek and Aramaic, the order of the games and the names of famous gladiators Herod had imported for the contests. Mithradas could hear the loud cries of the men as they made their wagers, waving their tablets of wax or rolls of parchment over their heads.

"Ten sestertii on Hermes!" someone called above the din. "Who'll take me?"

Hermes was a huge giant of a gladiator who had come from Rome and who had many victories to his credit.

"I'll take you," called someone else.

"Who'll take me, even money that Hermes loses?" cried a dark-faced Arab.

"How much?" asked an Egyptian near him. The bet was out of the ordinary.

"A talent. The fellow's luck can't last forever."

"I'll take you."

A loud roar from the lion pit at the far end of the amphitheater brought a sudden lull to the noise. Those lions had been brought from Africa to furnish the high spot of the day's sport. At the end of the contests two prisoners were to be thrown to the hunger-mad beasts who would tear them to pieces for the amusement of the spectators. As the roar subsided, the crowd turned back to the lists and read the names of the two doomed prisoners. Then the betting began again with more interest.

"Who'll take me, five sestertii to one, that the girl, Mara, dies first?" called a Roman wearing a brilliant orange toga.

"I'll take you," answered a Bedouin near by.

"Two to one on the boy, Judah," cried another.

"I'll give anyone an even bet that Judah dies without a sound," cried a swarthy Arab jingling his bag of money. "A talent if you'll go that high."

As a deeper roar rent the air a laugh rang out. "I'll

take you! I won't lose either, for the lion's on my side," said the man who laughed.

"Five sestertii to one that Judah tries to shield the girl," called someone.

"Even money that he forgets everything but his own skin when the lions are let in," a Syro-Phoenician from the edge of the crowd called to a friend.

The clatter of hoofs drew near and a cavalcade approached. A loud shout went up from the throng. The gladiators, accompanied by a military escort, were marching to their pits under the lower tier. Mithradas gazed into their faces as they passed him. Some were hardened, bearded men with the look of the killer in their small, deep-set eyes. Others, half-savage creatures, bore a stodgy, stoic expression on their dark faces, as if they knew their fate and would meet it calmly. Some of them, mere boys, clanked by with their heavy shields rattling against their greaves, their spears dragging the ground, a strained look of horror on their youthful faces. They were slaves, being sent to certain slaughter.

A wild cheer went up from the throng as they recognized Hermes. He swaggered by with his helmet pressed tightly down over his bullet-shaped head and his spear carelessly slung over his shoulder with his net.

The crowd followed them into the arena. As they disappeared through the gateway, another group approached. Mithradas noted that they were Jews. Their flowing robes fluttered about their sandaled feet as they drew near the lists. They stopped before them and talked in low, serious voices. Parts of their conversation were loud enough for him to hear.

"The boy Judah was a follower of the Baptist," one remarked.

"I've heard of Mara. She's a notorious courtesan," said another.

"But she became a follower of Jesus. They say he performed some miracle which changed her life," added another.

"Yes. She was with us on that last journey to Jerusalem."

"What crimes have they committed?"

"They're Jews. Isn't that enough?" a voice asked bitterly.

A lion's roar cut across their conversation and with grave faces they turned away.

"Has the Lord forsaken His people entirely?" Mithradas heard one of them say as they passed him.

"If we had any blood in our veins, we'd drive these usurpers out," an old man remarked as they drifted away.

As the hour for the games drew nearer and the throngs increased, Mithradas sensed a sinister undertone beneath the gaiety and the excitement. The Jews who went through the gateway wore grim, hostile expressions upon their bearded faces. There was no excited anticipation in their attitude and there was no reckless betting on the outcome of the sports. They had the attitude of those who went to witness an execution. Occasional snatches of conversation came to him from others who passed him, guarded remarks about Herod or careless jests which made him understand how thoroughly Herod was hated.

Nereus passed by and stopped for a moment to speak to him.

"I wonder if Herod is wise to have Mara and Judah cast to the lions," Mithradas remarked.

"What's the matter? Getting tenderhearted again?" Nereus taunted.

Mithradas ignored the taunt. "I've heard things since I've been standing here which made me believe that Herod has done a dangerous thing. Those two prisoners are Jews, and if he goes through with this it might cause him serious trouble. You know how upset things have been since the crucifixion of the Nazarene. This might lead to an uprising against Herod."

"What if it did? More Jewish blood would flow and there's plenty of that to spare."

"But Herod's position would be very dangerous. Don't you think he should be warned not to go through with this?"

"He'd go through with it even if he were warned. Don't let idle chatter upset you so much, Mithradas. You've been jumpy ever since Mara and Judah were condemned to the arena. If you weren't a Roman, I'd be tempted to believe you were in sympathy with the prisoners."

Nereus swaggered down the street toward the palace and Mithradas' troubled gaze followed him. *I wonder what he'd say or do,* he wondered, *if he knew the truth about me and why I'm so much interested in those two. I wonder what Herodias would say, if she knew the truth about me.*

In her room in the palace, Herodias sat tapping an impatient toe on the polished marble floor. A pale green robe of shimmering silk emphasized her dark beauty. About her waist she wore a girdle of darker green, studded with emeralds and pearls. Across her forehead and over the heavy masses of her hair were bands of emeralds and pearls. Her dark eyes were brooding and her unsmiling lips were drawn together tightly.

She could dispense with her conferences with Nereus now, for she no longer needed his aid, and his insistent demand for her presence just now irritated her beyond measure. When the curtains parted and he entered the room, she regarded him with a gleam of petulance in her eye. During the past months she had seen little of Nereus and she didn't want to see him now. The close contact with him caused disturbing longings which she had determined must be stifled with a firm hand. Every obstacle had been removed which stood between her and the throne she had set herself to obtain. The Nazarene had been disposed of and Herod had no reason to fear from that source. Pilate, once his enemy, professed to be his friend. It had made their carefully-laid schemes easier of accomplishment. Soon Herod would have at his command an army large enough to drive Pilate from Judea and establish the tetrarch as sole monarch of the land.

She was confident that none but the trusted few knew of the deeper plot to sever allegiance with Rome and to set up an Eastern empire of adjoining nations which would outrival Rome.

With such a future before her, she could not waste time longing for the presence of an ordinary palace guard, no matter how handsome he was, no matter how his love for her called to her wayward heart. He had played his part and served her well but now she wanted to forget what had kept him loyal. It was annoying to realize that she dared not refuse the audience.

She could not help comparing Nereus with Herod as he stood for a moment regarding her with reproachful gaze. His slim, well-built body was encased in a breastplate that glittered and shimmered from much polishing. His long mantle of crimson fell from his shoulder and hung about his sword scabbard in soft folds. His bold black eyes stirred her against her will. How different he was from the husband who had grown peevish and brooding! If only Nereus could have been in Herod's place! How often she had wished that!

"What do you want to see me about?" she asked coldly. "Be quick about it for I haven't much time to waste."

"You haven't always thought that time with me was wasted," he reminded her gravely.

"You know I'm in a hurry," she replied impatiently. "The games are due to start soon. Herod's likely to be here any minute. He wouldn't be pleased to find you here."

"You didn't mind his finding me with you in the past." His eyes held hers with a gaze which seemed to hypnotize her and it wakened fires she had believed she had quenched forever.

"That was in the past, Nereus. The past is best forgotten."

"You credit me with a very short memory, my lady.

How can I forget that past when the very games you are
to witness today are the result of my efforts in your
behalf?"

"The games are in celebration of Herod's birthday,"
she said curtly.

"I know. But the chief interest in today's sport is the
death of Mara and Judah. If it hadn't been for me, you
wouldn't have the satisfaction of witnessing her death."

"I think fate played the largest part in this affair.
Surely you didn't make the girl fall in love with this
fellow," she said sarcastically.

"You didn't give fate the credit for it when I first told
you about it," he said, with a cold light in his eyes.

"I'm not much concerned about the whole affair
now," she said indifferently. She turned away as he
advanced a step nearer and she saw something in his
eyes which made her afraid.

"You were very much concerned not long ago, when
you were afraid Mara would supplant you as Herod's
wife," he said with grim emphasis on each word.

"You enjoy reminding me of unpleasant things, don't
you?" she said angrily. "I have more important things to
consider now than a slave who has been condemned to
death."

"Are you sure these important things will bring you
happiness?"

"Quite sure." She stared at him coldly, for she read his
unspoken thought.

"There's the chance for many a slip before your goal
is reached. Don't feel too secure, Herodias."

"What do you mean?" She was struck by the subtle

warning in his voice which irritated her and yet filled
her with a faint fear.

He took a turn about the room; then he stopped
sharply in front of her. "What would you say if I should
tell you that your dreams of a kingdom may suddenly be
shattered?" he asked.

"I'd say you were very annoying!" she blazed. "If
you're trying to frighten me, you're a bigger fool than I
thought you could be. Now please go. I can't give you
any more time." She turned away and sat down upon a
couch among the brilliant cushions.

"I won't accept your dismissal until I've told you what
I came to tell you," he stated firmly.

"You're becoming a nuisance, Nereus," she said in
frigid tones. She took a flower from a silver vase and idly
tore it apart.

"To be sure I am," he retorted bitterly. "The faithful
soldier is no longer necessary to the plans of the tetrarch's wife. Naturally he would be annoying if he
reminded her that it was because of him that those plans
succeeded."

He advanced until he stood close to her and there was
a bolder light in his eyes than she had ever observed. It
frightened her unaccountably.

"You can't dismiss me that easily, Herodias. I came
here to tell you something that is for your own good. I
did it at the risk of arousing your anger. I'm doing it because I love you. The gods alone know why I do! Even
your coldness and your cruelty haven't driven my love
for you from my heart."

"I warned you never to say those words again," she

said as she rose and faced him. "If Herod should hear you, you might die with those others in the arena. His disposition hasn't improved in the past months and he's still jealous of me. Don't forget that!"

"Herod may not have the power of life and death much longer," he replied gravely.

"Just what do you mean by that?"

"His dreams of becoming a king may never be realized."

"He was never more sure of their realization," she stated. She hesitated a moment. Should she tell him the truth or wait and let him find it out when everyone should learn of it? She decided she'd tell him now. "A Roman army is on its way here to proclaim Herod king of Palestine and to see that he is established. Pilate will be deposed. Herod expects the army to arrive in time to make the proclamation when the games end today. The way to Jerusalem is cleared of every obstacle."

"Even such a small obstacle as Mara," he observed with a cynical smile.

"I shall not forget that, Nereus!" she cried sharply.

"You've told me that before, my lady, but your memory has proved distressingly short."

She flushed angrily at his words and her cold gaze traveled over him.

"I think it would be wise for Herod to have you transferred to some other duty," she remarked.

"My reward for faithful service to you?"

"For presuming too far."

"It is presuming, I suppose, for a palace guard to aspire to the love of a woman who expects to be a queen.

Yet you yourself gave me the hope that made me presume. It's because of the love you have constantly encouraged that I've come to warn you of the danger that threatens you."

"What danger?" she asked, with a note of contempt.

"The Jews are more upset than you realize over the fact that Mara and Judah are to be cast to the lions. They're in a dangerous mood. I felt it myself even before Mithradas called it to my attention. He's been watching them as they crowded about the gate of the amphitheater reading the lists."

"Do you expect me to be frightened because the Jews are upset over the deaths of two prisoners?"

"These two are Jews and it's the first time Herod has dared do a thing like this. You would have cause to be frightened if they should start an uprising."

"Why should I? They've had uprisings before and they've learned a bitter lesson every time. Perhaps they need one now, to teach them that Herod can handle the situation."

"Suppose Tiberius suspected that Herod is no longer loyal to Rome. You'd be caught in a trap between the hostile Jews and the vengeance of Rome."

Her startled gaze rested on him for a moment. "Tiberius would have no cause to suspect unless some traitor betrayed us," she said slowly. "If I thought you had done such a thing, I'd have you killed before you left the palace!"

He smiled at her brief betrayal of fear. "Do you think I'd be fool enough to have suggested such a thing if I had been guilty?"

"I believe you'd do anything to gain the thing you want." A grave expression settled upon her face.

"The only thing I want is to serve you. I came here to offer myself to you as I've done so many times in the past. I want you to feel that if any danger threatens you, I'm ready to serve you, even though you have scorned my love, even though you plan to send me away because I persist in that love."

"If the danger you suggest threatened, I'd need an army, not just you," she scoffed.

"If danger threatened, you could go away with me. I'd take you so far away that neither Tiberius nor the furious Jews could ever find you. You and I could be together, Herodias, and we could be at peace. You'd be far happier than you've ever been with Herod."

"You fool!" she blazed. "Do you think I'd go anywhere with you!"

He took a step nearer and bent over her. "You love me, Herodias," he said, in low, throbbing tones. "You can't deny it. You may be glad to come to me, if these dreams of becoming a queen should end in disaster."

She laughed a low, scornful laugh. "Don't delude yourself any longer with the dream that I'll ever be glad to come to you, or that I could ever know peace or happiness with you. The only peace and happiness I ever had was when I was Philip's wife. He was the only one I ever really loved. I gave up love and peace to follow the dream of becoming a queen. That dream will soon be realized, so you may as well know the truth now and forget any dreams you've had concerning me."

He stared at her silently and a faint uneasiness again

took possession of her as she watched his face harden and the cold gleam come into his eyes.

"If Herod knew some things you'd like me to forget, I don't think you'd ever sit on the throne beside him."

"Is that a threat?" she asked coldly, but the fear increased.

"Would a palace guard dare to threaten the queen?" he mocked.

"If you feel inclined to carry out that threat, you'd better remember what happened to John the Baptist," she advised in measured tones.

"I shall try to remember, my lady," he replied, and bowed with mock humility, then turned and left the room.

A sigh of regret escaped her as she watched him go. How foolish she had been not to have seen where this was leading her!

At the door Nereus met Herod coming in. He saluted the scowling tetrarch and went out. Herod turned and looked after him and the scowl deepened. No Caesar could have been more elaborately dressed than Herod was. He wore a royal purple tunic with a long toga of matching shade lined with creamy white. On his brow was the circlet of golden leaves which Caesar was accustomed to wear and on his arms were jeweled arm bands reaching halfway to his elbow. Today Herod was a king in his own eyes. Soon the people would know that he was a king in reality.

He turned to Herodias with a frown and a muttered oath. "So that fellow's here again. What brought him here?"

"He came to beg me not to send him away," she answered indifferently.

"I didn't know you had any idea of sending him away," and he stared at her in surprise. "It's a good idea, however. I'll be glad to get rid of him. I won't be stumbling over him every time I come in here. Why do you want to send him away? I thought he was one of your most trusted men."

"Can we ever really trust anyone?" she asked pointedly.

"What were you saying about John the Baptist when I came in?" he asked, ignoring her thrust.

"I was warning Nereus that a person may lose his head if he's not careful how he uses his tongue."

He turned away from her and paced up and down the room.

"I wish I could never hear that name again! I've wished a thousand times I had never beheaded John the Baptist."

"Must we go over that again?" she asked impatiently. "Don't be so childish about it. What you did was for the good of the land you govern. Forget about it."

"I can't forget him!" he cried in a distressed voice. "His face comes to me in my dreams to torture me. I'm afraid every time I remember that I killed him just for the sake of a drunken oath."

"That should teach you not to drink so much. If you hadn't made such a sot of yourself, you would never have given the oath."

"It was you who did it!" he cried furiously. "You made me kill a great prophet, just because you hated him."

"A prophet!" She laughed. "An upstart who tried to turn the people against you and keep you from your kingdom."

With a weary droop of her shoulders she approached him and laid her hand on his arm. "Don't let foolish fears spoil your celebration. It's almost time for us to be at the amphitheater. Have the chariot brought to the door and let's go and try to be happy. Today's your birthday. Think of the kingdom that will soon be ours."

"The *kingdom!*" he repeated as he started toward the door. "I wonder if a kingdom can make me happy when I'm so full of fears and unrest and regrets. Being a king won't make me forget!"

Chapter Twenty-seven

In the Arena

BY THE TIME THE CHARIOT OF THE TETRARCH ARRIVED at the amphitheater, the people were assembled in a noisy, expectant mob. The murmur of their voices sounded like the distant rumble of thunder as Herod and Herodias left the chariot and ascended to Herod's box. Banners were waving in rows of brilliant color and the bright armor of the sentries stationed at the various exits glittered in the sunlight.

As Herod entered the box, followed by Herodias and a few favored guests, the crowd broke into prolonged cheers. He acknowledged the cheers by raising one hand, palm upward, in the Roman salute, then sat back heavily in his seat.

The blast of trumpets sounded and the huge gates at the far end of the arena swung open to admit the first contestants. A dozen horsemen, armed with spears and shields, galloped from both ends of the arena to engage their antagonists to the death until the last man survived.

As the clatter of steel against steel sounded, mingled with the piercing screams of injured horses, the spectators watched with mild interest. This massed fighting lacked the thrill of the single combat, and these men dying out there upon the sands, now rapidly becoming red with their blood, were furnishing only the overture for the exciting drama to follow.

Herodias watched with brooding eyes. Her recent conversation with Nereus had upset her and brought vague fears. Nereus hadn't told her all he had come there to tell. What did he know that he had kept from her? Was there really danger that he had discovered or did he only suspect it? Suppose Tiberius should discover their secret of revolt? Suppose he already knew? Then surely that army so near the city would be an arm of vengeance and not the herald of added honors to Herod.

What a fool she had been to have talked to him as she had at such a dangerous time as this! Why couldn't she have waited until she was secure on that throne which had become such an obsession? Why had she ever left Philip for the bauble of a crown? If only she could go back to his arms, to the love she had once found so satisfying! Would this regret and longing always return to taunt her and add to her unrest?

The contest had ended and the victor, blood-covered and almost too weak to stand, tottered to Herod's box, where he stood waiting for the signal which would proclaim him victor. At Herod's whim, or the decision of the throng, he, too, could be slaughtered by the guards. About him were bleeding corpses and groaning victims in the last agonies of death. Injured horses were struggling frantically to rise and were screaming with agony.

Herodias turned her troubled gaze on Herod. He was staring stupidly at the scene before him. His face was pale and bloated, with dull purple spots showing through the pallor. Occasionally his hand swept across his eyes as if something obstructed his vision.

"What's the matter with you?" she asked in disgust.

"Nothing," he replied somewhat thickly.

"You've been drinking too much again."

"I haven't. I just drank a goblet of wine before we left the palace. It seems to have gone to my head." He brushed a trembling hand across his eyes again.

"It takes more than one drink of wine to make you as drunk as you are. You could at least have stayed sober until the games are over. This is no time for you to be drinking. That fellow down there is waiting for your verdict."

The wounded survivor raised a strained, anxious gaze to Herod's box. The tetrarch weakly extended one hand. It dropped inertly, thumb down, over the edge of the box. There was a howl of protest from thousands of throats as hands were waved excitedly with thumbs up and the spectators called to Herod to reverse his decision.

"Raise your thumb, you fool!" Herodias commanded in a hoarse undertone. "Do you want this howling mob about your ears just because you're too drunk to hold up your hand?"

Herod obediently raised his thumb while a wild shout went up and the survivor left the arena. Soon the horses had been dragged away, the dead and dying had been removed, and the sands were smoothed by large boards drawn by galloping horses and all was ready for the next contest.

As two gladiators entered the arena with their nets and short spears a shout went up from the multitude for they recognized Hermes as one of them. Herodias let her gaze wander over the throng. She observed the tier beyond, where a group of Jews sat. Their attention was focused upon Herod and her and their hostile gaze did not falter when it met hers. She wondered if what Nereus had suggested might be true. If there should be an uprising of these Jews just now, it would make matters more difficult for Herod in the beginning of his new reign. Perhaps it had been unwise to have sacrificed Mara and Judah to her vengeance. She was becoming morbid, she told herself, to let Nereus and his hints make her afraid when she should be thinking only of what success would bring.

A wild cry of surprise rent the air and she turned her attention to the arena. The unexpected had happened and Hermes had gone down before a younger and more alert opponent. The noise subsided for a moment and there was an interval of silence while the multitude weighed mercy against the lust for blood. As if at a signal from some unseen hand, thumbs went down and the audience shouted for the death of the favorite.

Herodias watched with impassive gaze as blood spouted from the wound in Hermes' chest and he writhed in his last struggle. People stood in their seats or strained far over the parapet for a better view of the gladiator's dying agony.

As the games continued Herodias waited with growing anxiety for the approach of the Roman army and the messenger from Tiberius who was to read the proclamation. Their approach was more important to her just now than the death of Mara and Judah. Not until Herod was proclaimed king would the small fear that Nereus had aroused be stilled entirely.

At last the final contest was finished. The arena was cleared and the sands were smoothed again. A trumpeter sounded a blast and the crowd grew tense with excitement. The lions caged beneath the end tiers seemed to sense what the signal meant and gave deep-throated, rumbling roars. An audible sigh, an involuntary gasp of horror, swept over the throng. People in the higher tiers craned their necks and leaned forward in nervous tension. Women closely veiled threw aside their veils so that they might have a clear view of the slaughter about to take place. Voices were hushed and a strained, weighted silence settled over the throng as all waited for Herod to give the signal for the opening of the huge doors at the end of the arena. It was through these doors that the two victims were to come.

Herod was staring straight ahead, with head bent forward as if he didn't see the throng waiting so tensely for the raising of his hand, as if he hadn't heard the signal from the trumpet.

Herodias turned her angry eyes on him and nudged him sharply. "You idiot!" she said in a sharp whisper. "Can't you keep your wits about you until this is finished? They're waiting for you. Give the signal and let's get this thing over with."

Herod roused himself with difficulty. "What signal?" he asked stupidly.

"The signal for the lions to be turned loose in the runway."

He rose unsteadily to his feet, raised his hand, then dropped lumberingly back into his seat. There was a blast from a dozen trumpets and the gate leading from the prison was opened. Surrounded by guards, Mara was led out into the sun-drenched arena. At every exit sentries prepared to withdraw before the signal was given for the lions to enter.

Mara wore a white robe falling to her ankles and held in at the waist by a white cord. Her long fair hair hung in soft ripples below her waist. As she stood blinking, the sound of quick, indrawn breaths floated over the silence of the throng. She looked like a bewildered child as she stood there with uplifted face, pale from the long imprisonment, beautiful and fragile as an alabaster statue.

At her entrance Herod roused from his stupor and leaned far over the tapestry-covered railing of the box. He stared at her with a fixed, intent gaze and a sudden alertness possessed him.

"She's more beautiful than ever!" he exclaimed. "And just as unconquered as she was the day I drove her from me."

"Herod, the people are waiting." Herodias was impatient.

"Nothing seems to conquer the spirit of these Jews," he murmured, as if he hadn't heard her. "She's too beautiful to be torn to pieces by those beasts," he added regretfully.

"Don't sit there staring at that girl as if she had you under a spell!" Herodias cried angrily. "The people are waiting."

He brushed his hand across his eyes as if to blot out the vision of Mara there on the sands before him. "What's the hurry?" he asked thickly. He rose unsteadily and extended his hand.

The doors opened again and Judah was brought in. He was clad in a short tunic of rough brown material. His black hair gleamed in the sunlight as it lay in a thick mass about his clean-cut face, now bleached to a prison pallor. As his eyes became accustomed to the light, he saw Mara. He flashed her a smile.

"I was afraid I wouldn't have the chance to see you again before the end," he said.

"O Judah!" she cried, "to think I've brought you to this! It's so terrible to know you're going to die because you loved me! I've brought you nothing but suffering."

"It isn't terrible since we're together, my darling. It would have been if they had taken you from me and left me alone. I wouldn't want to go on without you."

Mara looked about her for a moment, at the sea of eager, intent faces, at the doors where the chains were already loosened and from behind which the savage roars of the lions came. She turned back to Judah with wide, frightened eyes.

"I—I'm not afraid! I won't let them think I'm afraid! Do I—I—look afraid, Judah?" She tried to smile but her trembling lips refused to respond.

"No, my darling, not a bit. You're beautiful!" His

voice was low and tender. "You're like a pure lily among the thorns. Remember when I first told you that?"

"Oh, why do you say it now?" Her eyes were brimming with tears.

"It's what I feel, Mara, my dearest," he said solemnly. "I've learned many things back there in the darkness of the dungeon. All my doubts and fears about the past are gone."

"It was worth being in the dungeon to hear you say that!"

A savage roar again smote the air and the tense throng began to murmur in excited undertones, unable to stand the strain of the unexpected delay.

"Judah!" Mara cried. "Do you suppose it will—take—long—after they turn the lions loose—before—the end?"

"No, dear. Not long. When we see them coming, we'll just shut our eyes and then we'll wait 'until the day break, and the shadows flee away.' Remember that in a little while we'll be together again—for always."

"Together—for always! How wonderful!" she murmured.

Herodias gave Herod a vicious kick with her sandaled toe as he sat staring with wide eyes at Mara and Judah.

"Do you intend to let them stand there all day talking?" she demanded. "The crowd's getting impatient. Have the lions turned in. The people will think you're afraid."

The eyes he turned upon her were wild and glassy. He ignored her words but got to his feet and stood, clutching the railing.

"Bring the girl over here," he said to a sentry. "I want to talk to her."

The sentry crossed to them and ordered Mara to follow him.

"Good-bye, Judah." She gasped.

"Good-bye." He smiled encouragement as he looked into her frightened eyes. "Remember, we'll shut our eyes 'until the day break,' and then we'll be together again."

She followed the soldier across the arena with slow measured step that seemed to the waiting crowd the steady stride of a girl who was unconquered and unafraid. In reality it was slow and measured because her trembling knees refused to move faster and she was afraid that with each step she would fall. Her breath came in short gasps. She didn't want Judah to know how frightened she was, how she quivered with terror at the thought of the agony in store for them both.

She paused before Herod's box and raised her eyes to his bloodshot stare. Herod looked down at her for a moment and she fancied she saw a sudden soft light in his eyes. But he looked across at Judah and the softening light vanished.

"How do you like your condition now, girl?" he demanded harshly.

"I like it better than being your slave," she replied impulsively. She hadn't known she would say that, but the words seemed to be given to her and the mere speaking of them gave her a little more confidence, a little less fear.

Herod gave a start of amazement at her answer. "Do

you think you'll enjoy being torn to pieces by lions better than living in luxury as you could have done if you hadn't been such a fool?" he demanded.

"I'm ready to die, if it is God's will," she answered quietly. The answer gave her courage.

"Your god has nothing to do with it! You're dying by my will. You're in my power, not in the hands of any god!"

"You can do nothing without God's consent," she said firmly.

He laughed drunkenly. "I'm not a worshipper of your god. He can't do anything about it. All the gods on Olympus can't stop me."

"There is only one God, O Herod, the Lord God of Abraham," she said reverently. "He is omnipotent. He can do anything."

She didn't know why she answered him and prolonged the agony of waiting, but some strange power prompted her to answer his stupid boasting.

"If there is only one God, then why did you follow that fanatic who was crucified?" He leaned far over the railing, so far that he almost lost his balance.

"He is the Son of God. Even though you had him crucified, he rose from the dead."

"You're a fool to believe that!" He laughed again. "The God you worship has done nothing but bring you to your death."

"He's given me the hope of eternal life." Her voice rose in clear tones that reached every waiting, curious spectator.

"Eternal life!" Again his bitter laugh rang out. "Your eternal life shall soon be brought to a terrible end."

"It will be just beginning." Her voice was calm.

He staggered and almost fell and there was a burst of hysterical laughter from someone near by. He recovered himself, brushed his hand dazedly across his eyes and turned groggily to discover who had laughed. Then he turned back to Mara.

"While those lions are tearing you to pieces, you'll have time to think of where you could have been if you hadn't played the fool."

He uttered the words thickly and stared at her.

"I shall be thinking that today I shall be with my Lord in paradise," she answered confidently.

There was a catch in her voice, a gasp of fear, for a roar came from the lion runway. Herod laughed again with that same drunken laughter; then he stopped suddenly and swayed uncertainly, shook his head and brushed his hand across his eyes.

"Why don't you call on your God to save you?" he mocked. "If you'd ask him to, he might perform a miracle, just to show these people how great he is. That's what I'd do, if I were a god."

"Stop this foolishness!" Herodias said sharply. She pulled frantically at his robe but he didn't seem to notice her.

"I believe He could save me if He wanted to," Mara said, without taking her eyes from Herod's face.

"Fool!" he cried in a harsh, thick voice. "He couldn't even if he dared to try. No one can deliver you from my lions—not even your puny Jehovah!"

Mara's eyes grew wide with horror as she heard that sacred, forbidden Name upon the lips of this drunken Gentile.

"That is blasphemy!" she cried in shocked tones. "God will surely punish you for it!"

"Well, you won't be here to see it," he muttered in muffled tones. The fumes of liquor seemed to have burned themselves out and he slumped back into his seat with ashen face and trembling hands. He seemed like a stricken creature. Herodias shook him, but he paid no attention to her. His hands trembled and he shivered.

"Herod!" she cried. "Give the signal for the lions to be turned in!"

He stared at her as she repeated her command. A faint fear smote her as she saw his ashen face and purple lips and the glassy look in his eyes.

"All right, I will," he answered, with difficulty.

He rose unsteadily, attempted to raise his hand for the signal, then reeled and almost fell. He clutched madly at the railing and brushed a hand over his eyes with a violent movement.

"I can't see!" he shrieked. "I'm blind!—blind!" and his shriek ended in a hoarse, choking gasp.

For a moment he struggled to clutch the railing, then slumped backward on the floor, out of sight of the terrified throng.

With a frightened cry Herodias knelt beside him. "Herod! Herod! Speak to me! Speak to me!" she cried frantically.

Herod writhed convulsively for a moment, gasping for

breath, then lay still, with eyes staring wildly, with purple, swollen lips parted in a grotesque snarl.

"He's dead!" Herodias shrieked. "He's dead!" She began to wring her hands helplessly.

Terror seized the spectators and in a wild panic they rushed for the exits. In a seething, milling mass they struggled toward the gates. The cries of those being trampled and the frightened voices of the others made a hideous babel.

Herodias stood looking about her, dazed and terrified. She saw Mara and Judah standing in front of Herod's box. Judah had come to Mara and was standing by her side. Herodias' face became distorted with fury and for a moment she forgot her terror.

"Thrust those two through with your spear!" she screamed to a guard. "Don't let them escape!"

"No!" the guard called back. "I wouldn't touch them. Their god might kill me as he killed Herod." With a frightened glance at Mara he fled through the lower gate.

Nereus was suddenly beside Herodias. During the entire time he had been standing near but had wisely kept out of sight.

"What are you doing here?" she cried as she saw him.

"I thought you might need me. You have no one else to turn to now." He glanced at Herod's lifeless form. A faint stench rose from the body and it seemed as if worms were already forming in the still-warm flesh.

Herodias followed his glance but she turned away and covered her eyes with her trembling hands.

"Come with me while there's still a chance of escape,"

he urged. "If you wait too long it may be too late."

She let her hands drop and stared at him in horror and mounting anger. "I see it all now! That wine Herod said he drank before he came here. It had poison in it. And you put it there! You poisoned him! Now I know why you were so sure Herod's plans would never succeed. You knew he'd die before the games ended."

"That isn't true, but we haven't time to argue it now. Come on before it's too late." He tried to lead her from the box.

"I wouldn't go anywhere with you, you murderer!" she shrieked, jerking free of his grasp.

"Call me what you please, but get out of here while there's still a chance," he urged. "The Roman army is on its way here to arrest Herod, not to proclaim him king. Tiberius has been warned of Herod's plot to break with Rome. If Herod had been alive when the Romans reached here, he would have gone to Rome in chains and you would have gone with him. Do you want to go alone as a captive?"

"No! No!"

"Then come with me. And hurry! We have little time."

"Did you know this when you talked with me before the games?" she asked.

"Yes, and I meant to tell you then, but you only insulted me when I was trying to save you."

"You've had your revenge!" she cried, turning upon him fiercely. "You traitor! You murderer! You're responsible if the Roman army is really on its way here to arrest us. You're the one who betrayed us to Tiberius. I'm not going anywhere with you! Get out of my way!"

As if pursued by some unseen foe, she rushed toward the exit from Herod's box. Nereus followed her, a cynical smile of satisfaction upon his lips. He knew she couldn't go far without him.

Mara turned to Judah with an awed light in her eyes. The swift turn of events had left her stunned.

"Judah, it was the hand of God, wasn't it?" she cried at last.

"It must have been," he assented.

They stood there in uncertainty for a while as the shouting, struggling mass of humanity above them fought madly for the exits.

"What do you suppose will happen to us?" Mara said finally. She looked toward the huge door behind which the lions were roaring frantically, excited by the confusion above them.

"I don't know," he replied as his gaze followed hers.

They stood there tensely, waiting for what might happen to them, knowing the futility of trying to escape. Presently a guard came running toward them from one of the lower gates and Mara uttered a gasp of fright as she recognized him. It was Mithradas. The end was at hand!

"Come on with me while everything is still in confusion," Mithradas urged as he approached them. "The outer gate is open and unguarded and we can escape that way."

"Where are you going to take us?" Mara asked. There was but one fate to expect from Mithradas.

"I'll take you home with me until night comes. They'll never think of looking for you there. Tonight I'll help you get out of the city. Since Herod's dead, I don't think anyone will bother to look for you. Herodias has trouble enough of her own. Hannah is outside waiting for you. She came here hoping to get a chance to see you before they brought you into the arena."

Mara stilled the wave of joy which swept over her at the thought of escape. The memory of the trap Mithradas had helped to set for her made her suspicious and afraid. He seemed to read her thoughts.

"You can trust me this time," Mithradas assured her. "Don't be afraid of me, but hurry. Let's get away while there's still a chance, while no one suspects we're leaving. They'll think I was sent for you, if they're not too frightened to think about anything but themselves."

"Why are you doing this for us?" she asked, still skeptical.

"Because I, too, believe that Jesus of Nazareth is the Son of God. Herodias sent me to spy upon him but I learned to believe in him. Since you were arrested I've been trying to think of a way to save you. I can't forget that I was partly to blame for all you've suffered. Come on. Let's hurry. We'll talk about it when we're safe inside my house."

His words swept away her fears and suspicions and brought a new wave of joy as they followed him across the arena. Together they hurried toward the open gateway and to freedom. Mara took a swift glance at the empty box where Herod had so recently sat, baiting her. The weight of the past with its suffering and bitter memories, with its fears and disappointments, seemed to drop from her like a burden that had been thrown aside. Once more life with its promise opened before her. The love of life and the call of love surged through her like an elixir, bringing back the sparkle to her eyes and the color to her face.

As they passed the lion pit there came a roar from the excited beasts. Mara laughed aloud in sheer relaxation from the strain and tension of waiting for unspeakable torture.

"O Judah!" she cried. "We're free! Free! Can you believe it!"

"I'm trying to, but it just doesn't seem possible." He took her hand and drew her closer to him.

As they neared the gate she turned back once more and looked at the arena with the sun beating down upon it. A shudder shook her as she remembered what would have happened to them both, if deliverance had not come.

"Let's thank our God for deliverance," she suggested. "He's the One who made this possible."

The three of them paused and bowed their heads while Mara and Judah offered up a brief but fervent prayer of thanksgiving and praise to Him who had proved that He was able to care for His own.

"O Judah!" she exclaimed, as they went through the gate, "we're still together and we didn't have to shut our eyes even for a little while. See how beautiful the sun is! All the horror and darkness are gone! Isn't it wonderful!"

"Yes, my darling, it is wonderful! Wonderful!" he echoed, as he put his arm about her while they hurried down the narrow street after Mithradas.

Through the pattern of his mingled emotions, joy and relief, thanksgiving and new hope, there seemed to run like a golden thread the memory of those words he had quoted in the arena from the old, old song that was Solomon's and yet was Another's—"Until the day break, and the shadows flee away . . ."